# THE LAWLESS BORDER

It was just one year ago that the O'Hara brothers planned to buy themselves a ranch, settle down, and raise some stock. But that was before Milton disappeared the night after he won forty-four hundred dollars at a poker game. Certain that his brother was hijacked and murdered for his winnings, Lynn vows to investigate. When he arrives in Tucson, there's one man left on his list . . . and he finds himself face-to-face with the ugly muzzle of a six-gun!

# ALLAN VAUGHAN ELSTON

◆

# THE LAWLESS BORDER

*Complete and Unabridged*

# LINFORD
*Leicester*

First published in the United States of America by
Berkley Medallion

First Linford Edition
published 2021
by arrangement with
Golden West Literary Agency

A catalogue record for this book is available
from the British Library.

ISBN 978–1–78541–952–2

Published by
Ulverscroft Limited
Anstey, Leicestershire

Printed and bound in Great Britain by
TJ Books Ltd., Padstow, Cornwall

This book is printed on acid-free paper

# 1

The buckboard of Don Vicente Casteñada, with a canvas top sheltering its occupants from the desert sun, moved briskly across the border and made dust down the Santa Cruz Valley. A level plain of cacti and mesquite stretched either way to copper-colored mountains. Don Vicente himself held the reins while two armed *vaquero* outriders kept pace.

'We will stop for the night, *hija mia*,' he said to the young girl seated by him, 'with our friend Colonel Sykes at Calabasas.'

This would be their second night out of Magdalena where Don Vicente owned a large general store and a cattle ranch. Each fall he drove his teen-age daughter a hundred and forty miles north to Tucson, placing her in a select private school for young ladies for a nine-month winter term. Altagracia Casteñada was now a mature seventeen and this would be her last year there. Right now her delicate, dark-eyed face showed the fatigue of travel. But her voice had an eager lilt. 'I can hardly wait, Papa, to see Judy again.'

She spoke in English because she'd just crossed into an English-speaking land. Her Spanish world lay behind her. Judy Callahan, daughter of an influential Arizona cattleman, was her dearest friend. 'You will room with her again?' Don Vicente inquired. He puffed at a cigarillo wrapped not in paper but in covering from an ear of Indian corn. 'But of course you will. And when your school is over we must persaude her to visit us in Mexico.'

He whipped his team to a trot, holding the reins expertly with a gloved left hand. Clearly he was a *hacendado*, or landholder, of distinction and means. His narrow, sun-browned face, spiked with a gray goatee, couldn't have been more Spanish if he'd just landed at Vera Cruz with Cortez. The steeple sombrero shading it had a wide velour brim and his chamois-skin trousers had pearl buttons down the seams. A handsome, striped serape, discarded during the heat of the day, hung over the seat-back to his left while a short-barreled shotgun stood not far from his right hand. His outriders carried repeater carbines in their saddle scabbards. It was a normal way of life on this road called the *camino real*, from Magdalena to Tucson. Occasionally a band of Apaches was likely to slip away from the reservation to raid travellers on this trail. And worse, in Don Vicente's opinion, were certain renegade cowboys from the saloons of Harshaw, Charleston and Tombstone — lawless rowdies to whom any Mexican equipage was fair game.

*Sin verguenzas*, Don Vicente called them; meaning the shameless ones.

★   ★   ★

Colonel Sykes' new brick hotel stood out grandly among the dozen or so flat-roofed adobes at Calabasas. It was well past sundown when the Casteñada rig

3

pulled up and the colonel himself went out to hand Altagracia from it.

'Come and get it, *amigos*,'he greeted heartily. On the front steps a Papago Indian boy stood pounding a gong.

Bearing down on them from the north came a stagecoach which had left Tucson twelve hours ago and which after a meal stop here, would make the night run on to Magdalena. Its driver pulled up with a flourish, shouting: 'Make room for the Arizona and Sonora Mail and Express Line and six starved passengers. Thirty minutes for supper folks; everybody out.'

This was a relay station and a hostler came around from the corral with four fresh horses. The six southbound passengers included a hardware drummer, three miners, and a pair of cattle buyers hoping to find cheap beef south of the border. Don Vicente took Altagracia inside and registered for the night. The registry page he signed was headed: *Sunday, August 29, 1880*. A Mexican woman showed them to rooms at the rear of the second floor.

From her own rear window Altagracia could look out on a corral yard. It was a big corral with high adobe walls. In it were relay horses for the stage company, as well as teams and saddle mounts of guests stopping overnight. The girl saw the two Casteñada outriders, Pancho Morales and Luiz Pacheco, unsaddle their mounts, unhitch the buckboard team and turn all four animals loose in the corral. The two *vaqueros* then went to an adobe bunkhouse adjoining the corral where each could find himself a bunk for the night.

Altagracia freshened up quickly, not taking time to change her frock. From experience she knew that one must never be too late for supper at one of these stagecoach relay stations, else there'd be nothing left on the table. A last look from the window showed her a new arrival. He looked like a hard-riding gringo cowboy as he dismounted from a blaze-faced roan with four white stockings. He was tall and young and lean, wearing a six-gun, and cartridge belt. Quickly he off-saddled and turned his roan into the corral.

He hadn't arrived at the supper table when Altagracia Casteñada joined the company. Her father, who'd waited for her in the lobby, gave her his arm and took her in. The coach passengers and several overnight guests were already eating. All but one of them stood up until the girl was seated. The exception wore a checkered vest. The stone in his tie pin was blood red and shaped like the Ace of Diamonds. His face was bony, cynical, and a line across his forehead could be the imprint of the headband on a dealer's eyeshade. Ignoring the Casteñadas he kept talking in harsh, choppy phrases: 'Sheriff oughta do something. They're getting out of hand, them rowdies from Charleston and Tombstone. Shooting up towns; bullyin' barrooms; busting up card games; raiding trail herds; stealing the ranchers blind. Call themselves cowboys but most of 'em ain't held an honest job for a year.'

The stage driver agreed with him.

6

'You're right, Ace. They're gettin' plenty uppity, all right. In a county as big as this one, ain't much chance for Sheriff Shibell to ketch up with 'em.'

One of the miners put in a word. 'The worst nest of 'em, I hear, work out of Old Man Clayton's place on the San Pedro. Fast triggers like Gil Stilwell and Johnnie Ringo.' 'When it gets too hot for 'em on the San Pedro,' a cattle buyer added, 'they hole up for a while with the Curly Mix gang over at Galeyville, in the Chiricahaus.'

'Where the Tucson sheriff can't very well get at them,' Ace Shonsey pointed out, 'him being a hundred and twenty odd miles from Galeyville.'

'There's talk at Prescott,' the host Colonel Sykes remarked, 'of cutting that corner of the territory off from us and making a new county out of it. They'll call it Cochise County and use Tombstone for a county seat.'

'Which'd be good riddance of bad rubbish,' the stage driver said, 'even if they *have* got a couple of mountains full of silver over there.'

'Nothing'll help that end of the range,' Shonsey insisted, 'except a dozen or so outlaw cowboys hanging by their necks. They're worse than Apaches, them cowboys . . .'

He broke off abruptly as a newcomer entered to hang his high-crowned range hat on a rack and take the only vacant seat at the table — which happened to be beside Altagracia. Hat, riding jacket, gunbelt, and spurred boots marked him as a cattle hand. His gray eyes met Shonsey's but he didn't say anything.

In a few minutes the stage driver stood up. 'Feed time's over, folks,'he announced. 'We gotta be in Magdalena by mornin'.'

Reluctantly his passengers got up and followed him out. It left Colonel Sykes, the Casteñadas, Ace Shonsey and the tall *Americano* cowboy still at the table. In a moment they heard a whip crack and a jangle of trace chains as the Magdalena coach moved on south toward Mexico.

Presently the gambler left the room

and crossed the lobby to the bar. It gave the host a chance to speak confidently to his friend Don Vicente.

'In the name of my countrymen, Vicente, I want to apologize to you for what happened down near Fronteras. It fills me with shame. No wonder your people have such a bad opinion of us gringos!'

Casteñada's response came with grave restraint. 'Do not blame yourself, my friend. We in Mexico also have our banditti, our *sin verguenzas*. There has been guilt on both sides of the border. Some of our worst has gone to you. A few of your worst came to us at Fronteras. Your best is a vast majority whose manners and culture we admire.'He glanced at Altagracia. 'Do I not prove it by sending my daughter to school in your great country?'

'You are very generous, Vicente, not to hold the Fronteras massacre against all Americans.'

Altagracia of course knew what they spoke of. Of all the 'cowboy'depredations below the border none had been so fla-grant as a recent one on the Las Animas, near Fronteras in Sonora. A party of six-teen Mexicans, peacefully on their way to Tucson to purchase goods and carrying four thousand dollars for the purpose, had been fired on from ambush by a score of outlaws from north of the bor-der. Six of the Mexicans had been killed instantly. The other ten, abandoning the mules and packsaddles which held their money and duffel, had fled for safety to Fronteras where there was a Mexi-can military post. Few doubted that the killers were toughs from Galeyville and other Arizona 'cowboy'hangouts. One of the survivors claimed to have recognized not only Curly Max and Johnnie Ringo, but also Old Man Clayton and his three triggermen sons from the upper San Pedro.

The thought of it brought shiver of revulsion to Altagracia. 'I am very tired, Papa. With your permission I will go to my room.'

The men stood up as she left them. As

she passed the registry desk a slight curiosity made her glance at the book there. The gringo cowboy must have signed as the last guest to arrive. She saw his name on the bottom line 'Lynn O'Hara Cheyenne, Wyoming.'

He was a long way from home, the girl thought as she started for the stairs. Then she noticed a current issue of the Tucson *Weekly Citizen* on a lobby chair. She hadn't seen one since leaving school in May. Much must have happened since then. The exciting Fiesta of San Augustine would be going on right now. There'd be many parties and celebrations in Tucson, largest city in all of Arizona Territory.

The girl took the discarded paper up to her room. After lighting an oil lamp she sat down to look through it. Was there anything about Miss Silva's school, telling which of her chums would be back this fall? They'd quickly rejected her long formal name and had shortened it to 'Gracie.'

The only mention of the school was

the usual advertisement which ran automatically in late summer and fall issues.

A YOUNG LADIES' SCHOOL in TUCSON on Convent Street under the superintendency of Mrs. and Miss Silva. Tuition for nine-month term, $250. Boarders, $200. Day scholars, $30. J. M. Silva, Principal. Instruction in reading, writing, arithmetic, grammar in Spanish and English, religion and deportment.

The officers at Fort Lowell, an item reported, had last week given a ball at the post headquarters eight miles from town; many prominent townspeople had attended. Another formal dance would take place at the Cosmopolitan Hotel on Friday night, September third.

That, Altagracia calculated, was only five days away. Not that there'd be any chance for her to attend. They were very strict at the Silva school and a girl could go to a town affair only with an escort approved by her parents and the Silvas.

Another news item said:

Night before last four cowboys took over San Simeon by storm. They shot off guns and chased everyone out of town.

This was matched by a scathing editorial and it told the girl where Ace Shonsey had picked up his expression 'worse than Apaches.'

The cowboys are worse than Apaches. They ride into towns and take over with six-guns, make all manner of depredations. They are especially bad when they ride across the border into Sonora. They steal cattle in Mexico and drive them north for sale in Arizona. After which they steal horses in Arizona and drive them into Mexico for sale or trade, or to stock their mountain hideouts with.

There was the usual report of track-laying progress on the Southern Pacific.

The news revealed that construction had reached as far east as Benson by the end of June. Now the trains were running over the Dragoons to Wilcox and the track layers were pressing on toward the New Mexico line. By the end of the year the Southern Pacific promised to make connections with the Santa Fe near Deming.

Altagracia, schooled in current American history at Miss Silva's, knew that the Southern Pacific was reversing the usual process and was progressing from west to east. While all other cross-continental railroads were building *toward* the Pacific, the Southern Pacific was building eastward from California. The girl remembered the tremendous celebration on March twentieth, this spring, when the first train from San Francisco had arrived in Tucson. At the closing of the school term in May, Tucson had still been the eastern-most operating terminus.

Altagracia laid the paper aside and went to bed. Weariness put her quickly asleep.

At about midnight sounds from the corral awakened her. She heard a disturbance there and a snorting from the corraled horses.

It drew her to a window where she raised the shade and looked out on a moonlit corral yard. Four mounted men were in the corral and each had roped a horse. The night light showed their silhouettes clearly but not their faces under the wide-brimmed sombreros pulled low over their eyes. The corral gate was open and the four men rode out through it, each leading a lassoed horse.

A bold thievery, the girl sensed at once. Then she saw Pancho Morales, one of the two Casteñada *vaqueros*. The corral disturbance had aroused Morales and he came running from the bunkhouse in pants and undershirt and with a gun in his hand.

'*Parese! Ladrones!*' he shouted.

He let go a shot and one of the raiders whirled his mount to fire back. Altagracia saw Pancho Morales crumple in the dust of the corral yard and lie still there.

She saw something else. Morales himself hadn't altogether missed. His bullet had tipped the outlaw's hat askew and she could now see his moonlighted face. It was one she'd never seen before. She only got a quick glimpse because the man immediately spurred away in the wake of his companions. The four raced south toward Mexico, each leading a stolen horse. In less than a minute the night swallowed them.

For a moment horror froze the girl at her window. Pancho hadn't moved and she sensed he was dead. She alone had seen the face of his killer. Would she know it if she saw it again?

# 2

The northbound stage from Magdalena, after an all-night run, rattled into Calabasas and made its usual breakfast stop. At the hotel Colonel Sykes and his overnight guests were still at the table. A shocked girl who'd witnessed the killing of Pancho Morales could add nothing to what she'd already told them. 'There were four,' she repeated wearily.

'You saw only one face?' Lynn O'Hara prompted.

'Only one. An *Americano* face. He was the one who shot Pancho and I think he was their leader.'

'If he's caught could you identify him in court?'

'Perhaps. I cannot be sure.' Altagracia had been up most of the last half of the night answering similar questions.

'I got a wire off to the sheriff at Tucson,' Sykes told them, 'within an hour after it happened. By now he should be on his way here with a posse.' There was a crude telegraph line strung along the stage route for operating purposes.

Bleak sorrow for losing a loyal *vaquero* ruled the mood of Vicente Casteñada. Ace Shonsey's reaction was one of sullen anger because one of the four stolen horses was his own. Yesterday he'd ridden it here from Harshaw on his way to Tucson. 'The posse'll never catch 'em,' he predicted bitterly. 'Those devils had a five hour start in the dark and'll be deep in Mexico by now.'

Luiz Pacheco, the surviving Casteñada outrider, came in to get orders from his master. Don Vicente gave them in a tone of sadness, speaking Spanish.

'Listen well Luiz. We have lost a fine brave friend, you and I. He must be taken back home for burial in Mexico. You will guard his body till the sheriff and a coroner arrive in the afternoon from Tucson. After they have seen him, and have questioned all who are here, you will then put poor Pancho in our buckboard and take him back to Magdalena. My daughter and I will go on to Tucson by stage.' He turned to the northbound stage driver who had just come in. 'There is room for us, señor?'

The driver nodded. 'Happens there is. I only got three passengers and one of 'em can ride topside with me from here in.'

'I'll have to take the stage too,' Shonsey said sourly. 'Those thieving cowboys left me afoot.'

The driver looked at Lynn O'Hara. 'What about you, mister?'

The man from Wyoming shook his head. 'I had better luck. They overlooked my roan.'

A corral check had revealed that the four missing horses were Shonsey's bay, a sorrel saddle mount owned by Colonel Sykes, a brown pony ridden there by Pancho Morales, and one of the stage company's relay horses of rangy lines and a dark solid color.

Shonsey's eyes fixed with a malicious suspicion on Lynn O'Hara. 'Yeh, you're dead right, cowboy. They *did* overlook that roan of yours. I wonder why! Best mount in the corral — if I know anything about horse flesh.'

It was a barbed insinuation which O'Hara chose to ignore. He turned abruptly to Colonel Sykes. 'Soon as I pay my bill I'll saddle up and get going.' The cowboy left the room and Altagracia heard his spurs clink to the lobby desk.

The Casteñadas presently followed and a few minutes later their baggage was loaded on the coach. The main item was Altagracia's little brass-bound trunk. This was strapped to the rear boot by Luiz Pacheco.

A priest bound for the San Xavier mission and two Tucson merchants returning from a selling trip below the border finished breakfast and reboarded the coach. One of the merchants offered to ride outside to make room for the Casteñadas. The other one, together with the Casteñadas, the priest, and Ace Shonsey took the inside seats.

The stage rolled out toward Tucson, seventy miles to the north. The *Americano* cowboy on his blaze-faced roan had ridden ahead. Presently the coach caught up with him and for a while the horseman kept pace. From a coach window Altagracia watched him riding tall and straight in the saddle and she remembered a remark of Shonsey's at breakfast. Why had the thieves overlooked that fine big roan — the best horse in the corral?

★   ★   ★

The noon meal stop was Madera. There they met a Pima County posse heading south whose lathered mounts needed an hour's rest. The posse had been asaddle since shortly after getting a telegram from Calabasas during the night. Sheriff Charles Shibell himself was leading it and the posse included all of his available deputies except one.

'Is my nephew Arturo with you?' Don Vicente inquired as he met Shibell in the station office.

Shibell shook his head. 'Had to leave one deputy behind to mind the store. It

21

was Arturo's turn. He rode with us on our last coupla chases across the border.'

A rider of the Mexican constabulary would join this Arizona posse at the border and go along with it as escort. The same courtesy would be extended to a Mexican posse requesting to pursue thieves this way.

Altagracia heard and it gave her a sense of relief to know that her favorite cousin, Arturo Casteñada, for at least this once would not need to ride out after killer outlaws. Arturo was six years older than the girl and was now a naturalized American citizen living permanently in Tucson. For the past year he'd been on Shibell's staff at the courthouse.

The sheriff asked sharply, 'Did anyone see those horse snatchers?'

'Only my daughter.' Don Vicente admitted the fact uncomfortably. 'And she saw only one face.'

Shibell took out a notebook and led the girl aside to a corner of the station office. He motioned everyone else out of the way so that he could question her in detail and write down everything she'd seen from her room window.

Since the sheriff must ask many questions while feeding and resting the posse mounts, the delay here was sure to be longer than the usual thirty minutes. The station had a bar and Don Vicente felt the need of a *refresco*. He went in there and found Ace Shonsey with an audience of idlers. 'You notice they didn't touch that roan of his!' The gambler's tone was sharp with innuendo. 'Best horse in the corral, that roan, and they left it right there!'

A man down the bar prompted, 'You figure he was in on it?'

'Why not? He's a drifter cowboy, ain't he? Just like the rest of 'em. Looks like he came on ahead to scout the job.'

'Where's he from?' the barman prompted.

'Claims he's from Wyoming. But two weeks ago I saw him at Old Man Clem Clayton's place on the San Pedro. I was on my way from Tombstone to Harshaw and I stopped at Clayton's well to fill my canteen. And who do you reckon I saw comin' out of the mess shack? It was this same gunnie cowpoke who calls himself O'Hara. But that's not his name. Ike Clayton was in the corral yard and I heard Ike call him Jackson.'

'You mean he's in with that Clayton gang?'

Shonsey started to answer but checked himself as Lynn O'Hara brushed by Vicente Casteñada and came into the barroom. The cowboy faced the gambler with a quiet challenge. 'Go ahead, Shonsey. Tell them what you mean.'

Shonsey's mouth hung open and the skin of his forehead reddened outlining the mark of a dealer's eyeshade there. He looked down at O'Hara's holstered gun, then raised his eyes to meet a level stare. 'You was there, wasn't you?'he said sullenly.

'At the Clayton place? Yes, I was there. What about it?'

'Usin' a phony name?'

O'Hara nodded. 'The name Jackson. So what?'

Shonsey backed half a step away. He wasn't wearing a gunbelt but there was a bulge at his left breast and his coat wasn't buttoned. Lynn O'Hara saw the bulge and his hand suddenly reached under the man's coat and took out an armpit thirty-eight.

He laid it on the bar. 'Just so you won't be tempted, Shonsey. Same goes for me.' O'Hara drew his own forty-five and put it on the bar beside the other gun. 'Keep on talking,' he invited.

The gambler decided not to keep on talking. Instead he kicked hard at O'Hara's shin. The quick sharp pain of it threw the cowboy off balance for a moment. In that moment Shonsey snatched his thirty-eight from the bar and swung it to an aim on O'Hara. From the doorway Vicente Casteñada heard the gun roar and saw it sail across the room. The cowboy had recovered his balance in time to bat it from Shonsey's hand.

Then O'Hara's straight-from-the-shoulder punch landed on Shonsey's mouth. The man went down, spitting blood. He lay with his head on the brass footrail, apparently stunned.

Sheriff Shibell came charging in. 'What's goin' on?' he demanded.

O'Hara's forty-five still lay on the bar. He reclaimed it and put it back in his holster. 'He said I've been hanging out at Clayton's. Which is true. And using a wrong name. Which is also true. If you've got time to listen, I'll tell you why I was there.'

★   ★   ★

The noon stop lasted twice the usual half hour. As the stage rolled on north toward Tucson, Altagracia still didn't know what had happened in the station barroom. She'd heard the shot while answering Shibell's questions. When the sheriff left her to investigate, the girl had moved nervously to the elbow of a plump little priest who was on his way to the San Xavier mission. '*Que pasa, Padre?*'

The priest sighed. 'Violence my

daughter. Always there is violence when men wear firearms.'

In a moment Don Vicente had joined them. 'The sheriff,' he told them, 'is taking a statement from the *Americano*. He asks that I listen as a witness. You will eat with the good priest, Altagracia, while I attend the sheriff.'

Now they were rolling north again and this time Ace Shonsey wasn't with them. In no shape for travel, the man was laying over at Madera for tomorrow's coach. Again one of the merchants rode topside with the driver. The other one, a harness dealer named Bascomb shared the inside seats with the Casteñadas and the priest.

Again Altagracia looked from the coach window and saw Lynn O'Hara riding at the wheel, his strong roan matching the pace of the coach horses. 'Was it he who fired the shot, Papa?'

The *hacendado* shook his head. 'No, Gracia, he only saved his life by slapping a gun from the other man's hand. Then he told us a strange story which the sheriff believes to be true.'

'Please what is it?' the girl persisted.

'I also,' the priest murmured, 'would like to know.'

'Don't hold out on me either,' put in the harness merchant Bascomb.

'His name,' Vicente told them, 'is Lynn O'Hara. A year ago an older brother named Milton O'Hara left him in Wyoming and went to Tombstone. This Milton staked a silver claim in the Dragoons which he was later able to sell for ten thousand dollars. In Tombstone he purchased a bank draft for ninety-five hundred dollars and mailed it to a bank in Wyoming for deposit. Also he wrote his younger brother Lynn that he would go to Cheyenne by train and that they would then buy themselves a small stock ranch. For rail fare, and to see the sights of San Francisco when he changed from the Southern Pacific to the Union Pacific there, he was keeping five hundred in cash.'

'When did he write that letter?' Bascomb asked.

'In May a little more than three months ago.'

'At that time,' the harness man remembered, 'the Southern Pacific was only running as far east as Tucson. So to board a train the man would have to go by saddle or stage from Tombstone to Tucson.'

'That,' agreed Vicente, 'is what Lynn O'Hara told us. His brother planned to leave Tombstone at daybreak on May twentieth, on horseback, and sell his horse at Tucson before boarding a train for California. But alas, during the evening of May nineteenth he played poker at the Oriental Saloon in Tombstone.'

'And lost his carfare?' suggested the harness man.

Casteñada gave a thin, mirthless smile. 'No, his luck was the other way. In the game he ran his pocket stake up to forty-four hundred dollars. All in the barroom saw him gather in those winnings. Wyatt Earp, a part owner of the Oriental, advised him to delay his departure till the Tombstone bank opened in the morning so that he could bank his winnings. Milton O'Hara said he would think about it; then he went to his hotel and to bed.

'After a short sleep he decided not to waste five hours waiting for the bank to open. He had a gun and was used to taking care of himself. At the break of day he rode out of Tombstone for good. After crossing the San Pedro at Contention he headed for the Whetstone grade. On top of the Whetstones a Tombstone-bound stagecoach met and passed him. He exchanged greetings with the messenger and driver. That was the last ever seen of Milton O'Hara.'

# 3

Don Vicente took out one of his cornhusk cigarillos lighted it, and puffed it daintily. A window at his elbow was open and allowed the smoke to drift out on the warm desert air. By now Sheriff Shibell and his posse would be pressing on south to chase thieves and killers in Mexico.

'So his brother in Wyoming,' Altagracia prompted, 'has come to search for him?'

Her father nodded. 'After two months of silence the brother worries and travels to Arizona. During those two months the Southern Pacific track has been extended east to Wilcox and the Santa Fe track in New Mexico has been laid south from Albuquerque to Socorro. It leaves a gap of only two hundred miles between one end-of-track and the other with a daily stage spanning the gap.

'So by train and stage and gain by

train this Lynn O'Hara is able to reach Benson, only thirty miles north of Tombstone. At Benson he buys a roan horse which takes him to Tombstone where he arrives a month ago.'

'Which'd be two and a half months,' Bascomb calculated 'after his brother pulled out.'

'That is correct. At Tombstone the town marshal Fred White, and Wyatt Earp of the Oriental Saloon, inform him of Milton's last evening in town. They give Lynn O'Hara the names of those who were present in the barroom and who would know of the forty-four hundred dollars in cash carried by the missing brother.'

'That would include the Earp brothers and Doc Holliday,' Bascomb reasoned. Having sold harness in Tombstone he knew who frequented the Oriental.

'Also in the saloon that evening,' Casteñada told them, 'were some of the Clem Clayton group of outlaw cowboys; also an assortment of miners and drifters and a floating gambler named

Ubrecht. They could all know about Milton O'Hara's ride to Tucson the next day with a thick purse. When he got his list of names, the younger O'Hara set out to check them one by one. He must learn which cannot account for his whereabouts on the day Milton O'Hara disappeared.'

The priest squinted shrewdly. 'So that,' he deduced, 'is why the young man went to the Clayton ranch.'

'That is so,' Casteñada confirmed. 'The crew at Clayton's ranch seemed to be the most logical suspects because many border thieves and stage robbers have been traced there. Changing his name to Jackson, Lynn O'Hara went there and applied for a riding job. They do not trust strangers, but because they are lazy and hay is ready for harvest, they hire the cowboy for three weeks, just long enough to put up the hay. He eats at their mess, listens to their talk, learns nothing. When they lay him off he moves on to the next names on his list, a pair of miners at Harshaw.

'At Harshaw these two convince him that they have no guilt. It leaves three more names to be checked — two sheepmen at Arivaca and a man named Ubrecht of whereabouts unknown.'

'So O'Hara rode from Harshaw to Arivaca?' Bascomb surmised.

'Yes, señor. And at a sheep camp in the Oro Blancos near Arivaca the sheepmen prove to him their innocence. It leaves only Ubrecht on the list and one of the sheepmen remembers seeing Ubrecht.'

'When and where?'

'Coming out of Doctor Handy's office on Congress Street in Tucson with his left arm in a sling. The time is only a day after the disappearance of Milton O'Hara.'

Again Altagracia looked from the coach window and this time she failed to see Lynn O'Hara. To save his mount he'd dropped behind the fast-moving stage.

Bascomb nodded shrewdly. 'So the cowboy lit out for Tucson to see Ubrecht?'

'At once,' Casteñada assented. 'And last night got as far as Calabasas, registering under his right name. Tonight at Tucson he will search for Ubrecht.'

Altagracia had a thought. 'Perhaps Cousin Arturo will help him, Papa.'

'He figures,' Bascomb concluded, 'that Ubrecht maybe held up his brother and grabbed the forty-four hundred dollars. Milton wouldn't give up without a fight. So he could've nicked Ubrecht's arm with a bullet before Ubrecht drilled him.'

'It is the best likelihood,' Casteñada agreed. 'Perhaps Ubrecht and a companion rode ahead and waited in concealment for O'Hara on the Whetstone ridge. There perhaps they robbed and killed the missing man, hiding the body. If Ubrecht was wounded in such an affray, he must hurry on to Tucson for treatment from a doctor.'

★ ★ ★

35

There were two more relay stops, Sahuarita and San Xavier del Bac. At Sahuarita Lynn O'Hara caught up with them while stage teams were being changed. Bascomb had a question for him. 'One loose screw, cowboy. Seems like Shonsey was right on one count. That roan of yours *was* the pick of the corral. Why do you reckon the robbers didn't grab him?'

O'Hara twisted a cigaret, his sternness relaxing to a grin. 'You'll have to ask *them*. My guess is they figured a blaze-faced roan with four white stockings is too easily described and recognized. Horse thieves, I've heard, 'd rather run off solid colors — bays or blacks or browns.'

It was late afternoon with the sun hanging low over the Boboquivaris which walled the desert on the west. Looking east Altagracia could see the less bleak Empire Range to remind her that the ranch of her roommate's father, Mike Callahan, lay just beyond it along Cienega Creek. In another day or two she'd be rejoining Judy at the Silva school.

A station later, at San Xavier, the priest left them. A pair of swarthy Papagos replaced him and it crowded the coach on the last lap to Tucson. Again Lynn O'Hara, unable to change horses every twelve miles as did the coach, dropped behind.

On down the Santa Cruz river the stage rolled. The river bed was dry except that at every ranch a dam forced underground water to the surface, making in each case a slim pond with stunted cottonwoods along it. Otherwise there was little vegetation except saguaro cactus, ocotillo and mesquite. Just after sunset the coach turned into upper Main Street of Tucson between low adobe walls. They wheeled down a lane of small shops and cottages with window frames painted a bright blue.

At the Tully & Ochoa corral the stage veered a block east to Meyer Street down which it made dust to the Palace Hotel.

Last night's telegram had informed

the town of a murder at Calabasas and a curious crowd was assembled to meet the stage. Among them Altagracia saw traders, teamsters, saloon idlers, Indians, gamblers, riders from the valley ranches, and Mexicans from the *Barrio Libre*. Then she saw her cousin Arturo, handsomely young and with a deputy's badge worn proudly on his jacket.

With Arturo she saw an even younger man — a beardless, gangling fellow with tousled yellow hair. He was standing on the hotel steps looking straight at her. Then she remembered him. She'd glimpsed him a few times last winter sitting on a park bench when the girls at the Silva school were taking their daily exercise walk. According to Judy Callahan he was a boy who'd come out from California to take a job as cub reporter on the *Citizen*.

A man from the *Citizen*'s rival, the *Weekly Star*, was also there and with others he closed in on the stage company with questions as the Casteñadas got out on the walk. In the background

Altagracia saw one of her father's closest friends, Pete Kitchen of the Potrero Creek ranch near the border. A seasoned Apache-fighter, scarred and sun-baked, Pete Kitchen was sometimes called the Daniel Boone of Arizona. More than once the Casteñadas had stopped overnight at his ranch on their way to Tucson.

The veteran frontiersman met the girl's eyes and waved a hand. Then the hotel's proprietor, Fred Maish, pushed through to greet the Casteñadas as distinguished guests. '*Bien venida*, Don Vicente.'

'What about those cowboy killers at Calabasas?' the Star man demanded. 'We understand you saw 'em, Miss Casteñada.'

Getting through wasn't easy. 'She has much fatigue,' Don Vicente pleaded as he managed to get his daughter to the steps. There his friend Kitchen joined them and together they made a buffer for the girl as she reached her cousin on the porch.

'Hello, *prima*!' Arturo greeted buoyantly. 'All at once you are important, little one. From only a school girl of the *Mejico* desert you become, suddenly the state's star witness. And what a pretty little witness!' he added teasingly. 'Do you not agree, Roger Niles?'

Arturo spoke in Spanish but his hatless, yellow-haired companion clearly understood. 'I agreed,' he said boldly, 'since the first time I saw you taking a walk in the park, Miss Casteñada. But Artie is bungling an introduction. I am Roger Niles of the *Citizen*. I can see you are tired and it would be bad manners if I disturbed you now. Will you permit me the privilege of joining you and your father briefly at break fast? I will intrude only for a few minutes.'

The attention excited Altagracia. Had this nice young man really noticed her in the park, last winter? She looked questioningly at her father but at the moment he was occupied in exchanging warm and intimate greetings with Kitchen. It was the usual ceremony when a Mexican gentleman of rank met a friend after a long absence. To Vicente Casteñada the conventions of common politeness demanded it. He threw an arm over Pete Kitchen's shoulder and the other arm around his waist, following through with light pats on the lower back. The man greeted was expected to reciprocate, pat for pat.

Then each must inquire of the other's health and the health of his family. 'When I have taken Gracia to our rooms,' Vicente promised his friend, 'you must join me for a *refresco*.'

It all took a few minutes of time during which Roger Niles waited for his answer. Timidly the girl from Magdalena gave it to him. 'I do not think my father would object, señor.' That was as far as she could go. Anything like a solid date, made without parental permission, would have been unthinkable.

A new arrival was hitching his white-stockinged roan at the rack and a moment later he came up on the porch. A gun-weighted belt hung obliquely from his hips and the haggardness of a long, dogged ride was on his face. Vicente presented him at once to Pete Kitchen. 'He has come with us up the *camino real* from Calabasas. Señor Lynn O'Hara, I present my friend Peter Kitchen from Potrero Creek.'

The border cattleman and the tall Wyoming cowboy regarded each other with a shrewd respect. 'I've heard of you, Mr. Kitchen,' the younger man said. 'At Tombstone they told me you've fought more Apaches, and chased more horse thieves than any other man in Arizona.'

'It is true,' inserted Casteñada.

'Howdy,' Kitchen said bluffly. 'Anything I can do for you let me know.'

'All I want right now,' Lynn told them, 'is to look up a Doctor Handy. Know where I can find him?'

Anyone could have told him where to find the town's most popular doctor. 'He is a very good friend of mine,' said Arturo Casteñada. 'I will take you to him.'

'When?'

'*Mañana por la mañana. Temprano.* As you wish, señor.'

To rest his daughter as much as possible and to shield her from questions, Don Vicente had supper brought to their rooms. They were the rooms known as the 'Governor's Suite' and had accommodated such celebrities as General Nelson Miles, Governor John C. Frémont and President Crocker of the Southern Pacific. Originally the Palace had been a one-story adobe with dining room and bar facing the street and cot rooms at the rear. Later Fred Maish had added a second story and a brick front.

When a *mozo* had cleared away the supper dishes, Don Vicente went down to Join Pete Kitchen and other cronies at the bar. His nephew Arturo and Lynn O'Hara were there. The Wyoming cowboy accepted treat, more than once, and the tale of his search for a missing brother was retold. There were many *refrescos*. A youthful reporter named Roger Niles stood by with open ears and a notebook. He listened but asked no questions.

Questions would come in the morning, he hoped, when he took breakfast with the Casteñadas.

'Such a pretty little witness!' Arturo had remarked earlier. To Roger Niles of the *Citizen* it seemed an understatement.

At midnight the pretty little witness lay awake in her canopied bed, listening to the night sounds. It was a noisy town, this Tucson on the *camino real*. Dogs barked, horses whinnied, mules brayed. Windmills kept up their wheezy creakings while Mexican swains serenaded their *lindas*. Saloons and gambling rooms stayed boisterously open all night. From them came loud talk and sometimes quarrelsome bursts followed by gunfire. Men diced and died in Tucson while the church bells rang. Since March a new set of sounds had been added — the roar of trains which came pounding along the new Southern Pacific rails. The fighting cocks of such sports as Luiz Gomez and Maximum Zunego crowed defiantly at the approach of each dawn.

With all this were wheel and hoof sounds, firefighters pulling in and out, ranch help homeward bound after a spree, soldiers on furlough from Fort Lowell, miners from the lonely, silent places here to let off steam and make up for lost time.

All this Altagracia could hear from her canopied bed and after the quiet of her sleepy Magdalena, desert cow town deep in Sonora, they were exciting, welcome sounds. All winter long she would hear them from the room she would share with Judy Callahan.

In the morning her father would take her to the Silva school. But first there'd be a hotel breakfast where a young man with a nice face and yellow hair would talk to her about Calabasas. She remembered the way he'd looked at her. Did he really agree with Arturo that she was pretty? Had she been too bold, telling him that he could come?

The question absorbed Altagracia. And still the night sounds kept intruding from outside. The noisiest of them came from a distance — revelry from the San Augustine Fiesta going on west of Main Street, in a cottonwood grove by the stream. Once a religious festival, of late years it had degenerated into a gambling picnic lasting two weeks, night and day, where lower class Mexicans sang and danced or played with cards or dice. Others would celebrate in the cantinas of the *Barrio Libre*, at the south edge of the business district. People of her father's station never went into the Barrio Libre, which meant Free Zone. By tradition the *Barrio* people lived their own lives, lawless if it suited them and as long as they stayed in the zone the Tucson constables usually looked the other way.

The bell at San Augustine Church chimed again. Then Altagracia became aware of a strange and abrupt change in the street. 'Where there'd been noise, suddenly there was an ominous silence.

Then a shrill shout: '*Quedado, Alfredo*!' Watch out, Alfred!

From up Meyer Street came another

cry, this one in the voice of a woman. '*Quedado, Enrico. Tiene una pistola!*'

An Alfred and a Henry were being warned against each other; and Alfred, at least, had a gun.

The street silence tightened. Then the girl heard slow, converging boot steps on the board walk in front; two sets of steps approaching each other.

Then gunshots! Two of them, one from the right, one from the left.

A hushed moment and then a subdued voice — 'They are down — the both of them!'

A girl in a canopied bed shuddered. Had they killed each other? Why must men fight with knives and guns? Sometimes it happened even in her own peaceful Magdalena. She heard more shouts and running feet as constables and bystanders gathered at the spot.

The nice young man with the yellow hair, Altagracia thought, wouldn't see her at breakfast now. He'd be busy covering a Meyer Street shooting.

A street voice yelled: 'Bring a doctor.

47

Hurry.' So at least one of the combatants wasn't yet dead. Then it all dissolved into the normal night sounds of the town — the barkings, the whinnies, the brayings, the windmills, the wheels and the crowing cocks — and a bell from the church plaza.

# 4

A night sound which the girl could not hear was far away to the southeast in a canyon of the Patagonias. It was a click of hooves on gravel as two riders passed swiftly up the Sonoita in a northerly direction. The darkness of midnight showed no details of them except that one was short and thick, while the other was tall, lean and hatless. 'We've got no time to lose, Joe.' The hatless man spoke impatiently. 'It's a helluva piece from here to Benson; better 'n fifty miles.'

'We've got all night tonight,' Durango Joe reminded him, 'and all day tomorrow and until midnight tomorrow night. We can make it all right.'

A match flared as the tall, hatless rider lighted a smoke. 'We'll have to keep out of sight,' he cautioned, 'and get fresh horses at the Lowery pasture.'

'We've done it before, Luth.'

Twenty-four hours had passed since

these two men had helped the Lowery brothers steal four horses at Calabasas. Once clear of Calabasas they'd let the Lowerys ride on south with all four animals while they themselves had turned to push speedily northeast toward Benson. They'd already ridden more than a third of the way there.

Again Durango Joe spoke from the darkness. 'It worked twice before, Luth; so it oughta work this time.'

'It's *got* to,' muttered the tall, bareheaded man. 'Means thirty thousand dollars if we can make Benson on time.'

Durango gave a chuckle. 'It's a cinch the county sheriff won't bother us. Right now him and his posse are foggin' south after the Lowerys. He'll be across the border by now.'

The tall man puffed his cigaret. 'Some time late tomorrow,' he calculated, 'they'll find the four horses where the Lowerys abandoned them in some Mexico gulch. By the time the sheriff gets back to Arizona with 'em we'll be all through at Benson.'

'With our tracks covered,' chuckled Durango Joe.

This was a brushy canyon with steep, piny slopes. Near the head of it the riders pulled to a walk. Slowly they climbed to a divide and beyond this dropped into the watershed of Cienega Creek. Their route would take them down the Cienega a few miles and across another divide to the east which would put them in the valley of the San Pedro. The last dozen miles or so would be down the San Pedro to the railroad at Benson. All the way they must keep screened from the sight of settlements.

'We done it twice before,' Joe repeated. 'Both times all we got was peanuts. This time they's real dough waitin' for us.'

'You sure you got the straight goods on it?' the tall man questioned.

'Dead sure. That's why I rode all the way to the Patagonias to tip you about it. I knowed you was there tryin' to collect a gamblin' debt from the Lowerys.'

'Which I couldn't collect,' the hatless rider admitted sourly, 'seeing as the

Lowerys are just as broke as I am.'

'So you made 'em a proposition,' Joe said with a grin. 'You'd tear up the I O U if they'd snatch a few horses at Calabasas and use 'em to sucker the law into Mexico. And seein' as the Patagonias ain't far from Calabasas you offered to help 'em get started. No chance of the posse ketchin' up with 'em, is they?'

'Not a chance, Joe. The posse'll pick up the horses but nothing else.'

They pressed on and at daybreak came to the Lowery brothers' homestead on the upper Cienega. Except for a few pastured horses the place was deserted. In the cabin the tall man helped himself to an old black hat. He'd had to throw his own away on account of an incriminating bullet hole through it. After changing to fresh mounts he and Durango Joe rode on northeast toward the railroad at Benson.

★　★　★

When Altagracia and her father went down to breakfast at the Palace Hotel, Roger Niles of the *Citizen* was waiting for them. He was discreet enough to address himself first to Don Vicente.

'Sir, your nephew Arturo is my very good friend. He has shown me your report on the Calabasas affair. I have two questions — one for the young lady and one for you. Have I your permission to ask them?'

Don Vicente was impressed by his politeness and restraint. 'You will join us at coffee?' He motioned Roger Niles to a seat. They were at a private table in a corner of the dining room. A long table at the center had a dozen regular boarders. The reporter sat down and a waitress filled his cup.

'About the last man out of the corral,' he said to Altagracia. 'Your report mentioned him as the leader. May I ask why?'

She couldn't be sure about it. But somehow the man had impressed her as being more important than the others. 'As they came out with the stolen horses,' she remembered, 'he waved an arm at the others as though giving orders. He pointed in a certain direction as though telling them which way to go.'

Roger Niles gave a brisk nod. 'And they went that way while he himself was ment to deal with Morales.'

'I think,' the girl offered timidly, 'that there is a bullet mark on his hat.'

An intruding voice spoke up. 'She's quite right, Uncle Vicente.' Deputy Arturo Casteñada had approached the table with Lynn O'Hara. Arturo had a telegram in hand. 'The sheriff sends it,' he announced, 'from the first wire station beyond Calabasas. It is a border station which they will some day call Nogales. A mile or so beyond Calabasas picked up a hat with a bullet hole through the rim. Your leader threw it away, Gracia, so that he will not be seen wearing it.'

Roger Niles asked keenly, 'Does it have a dealer's label?'

The deputy nodded. 'It was purchased at the Allen store in Tombstone. A range Stetson, like hundreds of others. We will ask Marshal White at Tombstone to see if there is a record of the buyer.'

'He will be of the shameless ones,' Vicente Casteñada predicted, 'who steal on both sides of the border. Have you had breakfast, Arturo?'

His nephew nodded ruefully. 'Much to my discomfort. This early rising cowboy had me up an hour ago so that we can see Doctor Handy.'

'I have to check on a guy named Ubrecht,' Lynn O'Hara explained, 'before he finds out I'm in town looking for him.'

'I'll go along with you,' Roger Niles decided briskly. At the bar last night he'd learned all about Lynn's search for a missing brother.

'You had a question for me?' Vicente reminded him.

Niles put it at once. 'It is not a question, Mr. Casteñada, but a theory of mine and I want to see if you agree. Four months ago Sheriff Shibell's posse chased stock thieves across the border and didn't catch them. Two months ago it happened again, you remember?'

'I remember quite well. So?'

'In each case there was a stage robbery by masked men on the Tombstone-Tucson road. In each case it happened while the sheriff's crew was seventy miles away chasing stock thieves in Mexico. The stage loot in each case was of small consequence. In one case a Wells Fargo messenger was wounded. My question is, could it be coincidental? Or was it planned? Do stage bandits north of the border arrange to lure Arizona lawmen south of the border to make stage robbers safe from pursuit? If so, is this affair at Calabasas another such scheme of diversion?'

Don Vicente stared vacantly for a moment. He wouldn't have believed this gangling youngster capable of such shrewd reasoning. 'It is difficult to know,' he murmured, then turned to Lynn O'Hara who was still standing. 'What do you think, señor?'

The cowboy from Wyoming mulled it over. 'Could be,' he admitted. 'Stealing four seventy-five dollar horses bold like that would hardly be worth the risk — unless they had another deal on the side. If we hear of a stage job up north while the sheriff's in Mexico it'll look like Arturo's got the slant. Look, fella. Doc Handy oughta be in his office by now. Ready?'

Arturo was ready but reluctant. He liked to linger in pleasant company. '*Hasta luego*, Uncle Vicente. And you too, my little cousin. You will enter the school today?'

'Papa will take me there.' The girl spoke to Arturo but looked shyly at Roger Niles.

'Your friend Judy Callahan was in town shopping last week,' Roger said. 'She told me she's expecting you. Hate to rush off like this. Got to make a living. Thanks and so long, Don Vicente. Happy school days, Miss Casteñada.'

★ ★ ★

Doctor Handy's office was at the top of shabby steps on Congress Street. He'd

57

just opened it for the day when Arturo came in with Lynn O'Hara and Roger Niles. The doctor was a square-cut, kindly man with gray sideburns. 'What can I do for you, boys?'

'I'm lookin' for a man named Ubrecht,' Lynn told him. 'Last seen he was coming out of your office with a fresh arm bandage. The date was around May 21st or 22nd. Was it a bullet wound?'

Handy went to his record book and looked up the case. 'A gun wound,' he confirmed. 'Said he was cleaning his gun and it went off. Maybe. There was an amateur bandage around the wound which he couldn't have wrapped and tied himself. Someone was either with him at the time he was shot or shortly afterward. The bandage had been cut from the sleeve of a white linen shirt. The wounded man wore a gray woolen shirt.'

'You asked him who tied the bandage?'

'Yes. He said it was a teamster he met on the road to town. Said he didn't know the man. Gave the name of Ben Ubrecht.

I charged him six dollars and he handed me a twenty. I gave him the change and he left.'

'How fat was the roll he stripped the twenty off of?'

'I didn't notice.'

'He was dead broke, according to Wyatt Earp, two nights earlier when he quit a card game at Tombstone. Then he rides to Tucson and gets here with at least twenty bucks. Did he give a Tucson address?'

Handy shook his head. 'But a few days later I saw him go into Gary's bar.'

Gary's saloon was on the other side of Congress at the Court Street corner. The three young men went there and learned that Ben Ubrecht had a room over the barroom. The man had lived there since late May but at the moment he was out.

'I'll wait for him,' Lynn decided'. He took a seat in the corner and prepared to wait patiently. It was an untidy bar with a sawdust floor. Customers were talking about a gun-fight on Meyer Street last night.

'They quarreled over a woman,' a man said.

Arturo and Roger waited with Lynn for an hour or so. Then the deputy had to check affairs at the courthouse and the reporter had to do the same at his paper. It left O'Hara waiting alone there. Ubrecht was the last name on his list and there was a strong circumstantial count against him. Had he robbed Milton O'Hara of forty-four hundred dollars at the expense of an arm wound?

At noon Lynn went to the Palace Hotel for a quick lunch and found that Don Vicente had taken his daughter in a carriage to install her at the Silva school. Arturo came in with a report. The sheriff and his crew were still below the border, co-operating with Mexican authorities. 'There is no news of a stage robbery up this way' Arturo said. 'So the thought of a diversion at Calabasas seems to be wrong.'

'Maybe the returns aren't all in yet,' Lynn said.

He hurried back to the Gary saloon

to resume his watch. The afternoon dragged by and Ubrecht didn't come. *Maybe he's heard I'm looking for him. If he's got Milton's money on him, he'd duck out.*

When Lynn went to the Palace for supper Roger Niles joined him there. 'Do me a favor, Roger. Check the livery stables and see if Ubrecht has a horse in town. If you find he has, let me know at Gary's bar.'

He went back to Gary's to watch and wait. The place filled up noisily with teamsters, ranch hands, town clerks and Congress Street idlers. They were mostly *Americanos* because this wasn't one of the town's Mexican quarters. Lynn heard talk of the Calabasas murder and other depredations made by outlaws referred to loosely as 'cowboys.' He didn't like to hear the term used that way because he himself was a cowboy.

By eleven in the evening Ben Ubrecht still hadn't put in an appearance. Then Roger Niles came along with a report. 'Another telegram from the sheriff. It

61

just came in from a station below the border. The posse caught up with those four stolen horses.'

'What about the four horse thieves?'

'No sign of them. Looks like they got leery and abandoned the horses. The posse found 'em grazing loose in a gulch fifteen miles deep in Mexico. Hoofprints show that only two of the thieves were with 'em when they dropped the stolen stock. Shibell's still following those prints. Likely he'll lose 'em in the rocks.'

'You checked the local livery barns?'

Roger nodded. 'No horse of Ubrecht's in any of them. But this town's got lots of private corrals and sheds where he could keep his horse. I checked the eastbound Southern Pacific train too, that just went through, in case Ubrecht tried to duck out on it. He didn't. Saw the Southern Pacific paymaster, though, on his way to pay off construction crews strung out from end-of-track to the New Mexico line. Tomorrow's the first of September, pay day for five or six hundred graders and track-layers.'

Lynn was absently interested. 'This paymaster has the pay money with him?'

'No. He picks it up at midnight as the tram goes through Benson.'

# 5

It was nearly midnight at Benson, the brand new railroad station forty-odd miles east of Tucson. A train was soon due from the west. A few people were on the dark platform waiting either to meet arrivals or to board the train. It would only run another forty miles east, to Wilcox, at present the operating end of the line.

There'd been no Benson until three months ago when the Southern Pacific had chosen this spot to cross the San Pedro River. Now the place had four hundred people, a water tank and depot, a street of frame business houses, and a small brick bank.

In a half-finished store building next to the bank two masked men stood quietly waiting. The taller of the two wore a non-descript range hat he'd picked up at the Lowery brothers shack on Cienega Creek. Just forty-eight hours had passed since a raid on a hotel corral at Calabasas.

The stockier man smiled behind his mask. 'You reckon the sheriff's still in Mexico?'

'Maybe. Or he could be heading back by now. But he's still too far away to bother us any.'

More minutes slipped by while they listened for the sound of a train whistle coming this way from the west. All they could hear was a hum of voices from the depot platform, the clicks of a telegraph set in the operator' room, and the champing of two saddled horses at a nearby hitchrail.

The taller man shifted restlessly. 'You sure you got the right dope on this, Joe?'

'Dead sure, Luth. Mercedes heard the banker tell his wife about it.'

It reassured Luth. He knew that Mercedes was Durango Joe's current *querida* and that she was also cook at the house of the Albert Marburys. Marbury had just opened the new bank here at Benson — the bank nearest to the end of

Southern Pacific track construction.

'It'll be a pushover,' Durango promised. 'The pay moneys in Marbury's vault waiting for the Southern Pacific paymaster to pick it up. In a few minutes he'll get off the train and wait at the coach steps. Soon as the train stops Marbury and a guard'll come out of the bank with the bag of cash. They figure to walk across the street with it, hand it to the paymaster who gets back on the train with it. The train scoots on to end-of-track at Wilcox where a flock of contractors are waiting. Grading, track-laying and bridge-building contractors. The paymaster divides the money among 'em and then each contractor drives on east by rig to pay off his crew in the morning.'

'In all,' Luth calculated, 'enough dough to pay five or six hundred men for a month's work. It can hardly be less than thirty thousand.'

Now they could hear the rumble of wheels from an oncoming train. It was exactly midnight. Half an hour ago they'd seen Marbury and his armed guard go into the bank. Presumably the two men were now waiting just inside the bank's bolted door. 'We'll take 'em,' Luth whispered, 'when they step out on the walk.'

It wasn't a board walk, only a path of tamped cinders. Benson was much too new and raw for such improvements as paint or street lamps or wooden side-walks.

The engine's headlight made a sweeping glare as it came around a curve of track. This train had been arriving at midnight since late in June and those waiting at the depot had no reason to think a money delivery would be made at the stop here. The secret, except for Mercedes' confidence to Durango, had been well kept. Pima County had not yet installed a deputy at Benson. The town's storekeepers had appointed a local con-stable but more than likely he was at home in bed.

The train puffed in and clanked to a hissing stop. A few people got off. At the same time a door bolt clicked at the

bank and the door opened. Banker Marbury came out with a satchel and with
an armed guard flanking him. Seventy
steps would take them to a paymaster on
the depot platform.

They'd taken only three of those steps
when guns punched into their backs.
'Drop it!' a voice ordered. The cocking
of two gun hammers made clicks.

Marbury froze and dropped the
satchel. The guard half turned, started
to reach for his gun, then he too froze.
There was no outcry. People at the depot
across the street could have no idea of
what was going on.

'Go to sleep,' Durango said softly. He
hit hard at the guard's skull with the barrel of his forty-five. The guard fell flat to
the dust, still without any outcry. The
street was a curtain of darkness screen-
ing them from the depot.

It left Marbury erect, petrified with
panic and with a gun still punching his
spine. Luth used his free hand to pick up
the satchel. Then he gave the banker a
shove which sent him sprawling headlong

into the street.

'I better put *him* to sleep too,' Durango Joe muttered. Again he hit with the gun barrel and the blow stunned Marbury. The gun was cocked and the jar made it go off. The bullet went harmlessly into the dust but the boom of the shot brought cries of alarm from the depot.

Two masked men raced to a hitchrail and swung into saddles. Half a minute later they were speeding south out of town.

Five minutes after that they splashed into riffles of the San Pedro. After riding a mile or so upriver they emerged into a band of range cattle which had bedded down for the night along the water. At daybreak the cattle would get up to graze, spreading this way and that, tramping out hoofprints in the shore sand.

It was still five hours till daybreak and even then there could be nothing but a makeshift and amateur pursuit. 'They'll telegraph Tucson,' Joe chuckled. 'Nobody at the sheriff's office but a kid deputy named Casteñada. Where do we divvy up, Luth?'

'At the sheep camp. Nobody there this season.' The taller man relaxed and rolled himself a brown paper cigaret.

The sheep camp was a rock shack about nine miles south-west of Benson and north of Apache Peak. A herder had left a lantern there and by its light the loot was quickly counted. 'Thirty-two thousand, Joe. Take your cut and get going.'

They parted, each man riding off with sixteen thousand dollars in payroll-size currency. Durango would go straight to his little ranch on the San Pedro a few miles north of Contention. Like a dozen other shoestring 'ranches' in south-eastern Arizona, it was only a hole-up from which raids were occasionally made on stagecoaches, pack trains or stock pastures. The most notorious of these was the Clem Clayton place further upriver, above Charleston. Durango Joe had had connections with all of them. Sometimes he'd ridden with the Clayton bunch, sometimes with Tombstone or Galeyville toughs under Curly Max or Johnnie Ringo.

But of late his favorite and more discreet alliance had been with Luther Ward Larabee whose L Bar ranch on the lower Cienega had a respectable reputation.

No one was likely to suspect Larabee. The best people of the county were his friends. He stood high with reputable stock-men like Colonel Hooker and Pete Kitchen and Mike Callahan. He was handsome and twenty-five, and mothers with marriageable daughters weren't overlooking him. He was a popular dinner guest among the upper crust Tucson families, both Spanish and *Americano*, trusted alike by such citizens as Estavan Ochoa and ex-governor Safford. Durango remembered with a grin that Larabee had once ridden with one of Sheriff Shibell's posses on a chase after stage robbers into the Santa Catalina Mountains.

★ ★ ★

Ward Larabee, riding through his own ranch gate at daybreak, knew a feeling of security for the first time in a year. His L Bar outfit was mortgaged, every horn and acre to the Safford bank in Tucson and the note was overdue. Now, as soon as the hue quieted down, he could pay interest and a chunk on the principal, enough to forestall foreclosure.

His cabin was empty and there was no sign of a caller during his absence. No one could prove he'd been away for four days and nights. He'd given the Mexican couple who worked for him a week off to attend the Feast of San Augustine at Tucson, twenty-two miles west of here.

Nor did the world of Tucson know anything about his association with the Lowerys and Durango-Joe Dawson. As for other cowboy outlaws along the San Pedro Larabee had never associated with them at all. Durango kept him informed about them and sometimes he knew of their plans. But they, he was sure, knew nothing of his.

In the cabin Larabee made a fire and

recounted the money. He put it in a metal box and hid it under a floorboard. Then he fed himself and went to bed. He'd been in the saddle for most of four days and nights and it left him bone-weary. There was an important social event coming up in Tucson on Friday night and he must rest for it.

Before slipping into sleep he reviewed everything to reassure himself. This last coup seemed safe enough. But what about matters before that?

His mind delved back to Wichita, Kansas, where, five years ago at the age of twenty, he'd killed a man in a street fight. From that trouble he'd escaped to Texas where he'd punched cows till 1877 and then had helped take a trail herd to Camp Grant, Arizona Territory, where the government had to feed Indians on the San Carlos Reservation. Hearing of a ranch for sale on Cienega Creek he'd bought it with a small down payment.

Right away he'd made friends with a prosperous neighbor upcreek, Mike Callahan of the Circle C. He'd helped

Callahan stand off a band of raiding Apaches and it had won him the stockman's warm gratitude. Mike Callahan had introduced him to the best people at Tucson. Later Larabee had borrowed money from the Safford bank to buy cattle and more land. It had involved him over his depth and he'd become desperate for cash.

Then a drifter he'd known in Kansas had come along — Durango Joe, who knew of the Wichita killing. Joe had hailed Larabee as 'Luth,' although since leaving Kansas Larabee had dropped the name Luther and was known only as Ward Larabee. Durango, who'd been running with the Curly Max gang upon occasion, had now filed a land claim on the San Pedro and was using the place as a base for petty raiding.

'Bunch of Charleston cowboys,' he informed Larabee in April, 'just stole some Arizona steers and drove 'em into Mexico for sale. Sheriff Shibell and every deputy he can scrape up has gone chasin' after 'em.'

Which had given Larabee his big idea. Stages running between booming Tombstone and Tucson sometimes carried shipments of Wells Fargo cash and bullion. With the sheriff's crew away in Mexico, right now would be a good time to hold up a stage.

'We'd need help,' he'd suggested to Durango Joe.

'I know three guys camped not far from here, Luth. Fella named Ubrecht and a coupla brothers named Lowery.'

With the Lowerys and Ubrecht they'd held up a Tombstone stage with disappointing results. The take had netted them barely a hundred dollars apiece. A second Job in June, at the next absence of the sheriff's crew on a chase into Mexico, had brought them only a little more than that. Not nearly enough to make a dent in Larabee's debts or to keep up his social front in Tucson.

Until last night's payroll cleanup his only worthwhile job to date had been one he'd handled on the side with Ben Ubrecht, without Durango or the Lowerys

75

knowing anything about it. Ubrecht's wanton killing of the victim had drawn a rebuke from Larabee. There'd been no sense in it. After hiding the body he'd split the take with Ubrecht and sent the man packing for keeps. Since then he'd not seen Ubrecht and hoped he never would again.

And now, Ward Larabee promised himself before slipping into sleep he could also shuck off the Lowerys and Durango. With sixteen thousand dollars he could square his accounts and make a fresh start. No use taking any more chances. Mike Callahan had a good looking daughter coming along — and no other heirs. Why not go straight from now on and marry the Circle C?

# 6

Lynn O'Hara wakened lazily in his room at the Palace Hotel. Sunlight and the noises of Meyer Street came in through his open window. He still needed sleep after sitting up till well past midnight in Gary's saloon waiting vainly for the return of Ubrecht.

A wall calendar reminded Lynn that today was Wednesday, September first of the year 1880. A private school for young ladies opened today and yesterday Vicente Casteñada had delivered his daughter there. Today the *hacendado* would be catching a stagecoach back to Mexico.

His own job, he remembered as he got out of bed, was to keep nose down on the track of Ubrecht. Lynn dressed hurriedly, washed and shaved at the room's china bowl and mirror.

A dozen men were breakfasting when he entered the dining room. One of them had bruised lips and his face took an angry flush at sight of the cowboy from Wyoming. He was the gambler Ace Shonsey who'd laid over a day to recuperate at Madera station. He could have arrived in Tucson by last evening's stage.

Others at the table included Pete Kitchen, Vicente Casteñada, Mayor Leatherwood, City Marshal Ike Brokow, and the territory's leading freighter, Estavan Ochoa. They were in excited talk about a telegram which had arrived during the night from Benson. 'They got clean away with it!' Brokow was exclaiming. 'A thirty-two thousand dollar pay satchel! And nobody to chase 'em except a crowd of mixed-up small-towners.'

'They say Marbury didn't even see them,' Leatherwood added. 'The guard half turned his head and got a snap look. Two masked men, one tall and slim, the other thick and short. All happened in half a minute.'

'And the sheriff's crew eighty miles away!'

Vicente Casteñada recalled a theory

offered by young Roger Niles of the *Citizen*. 'Three times it has happened that way!' he murmured. 'I wonder! Good morning, Señor O'Hara.'

Lynn joined them and the news from Benson made him forget Shonsey. A smouldering gleam in the gambler's eyes indicated that he wasn't forgetting O'Hara. His mouth was still swollen from the punch at Madera.

'Nobody at the sheriff's office except that young nephew of yours,' Ike Brokow remarked to Don Vicente. 'He's got orders to mind the shop till Shibell gets back. It's a cinch I can't spare any of my town force for a chase job — not with the *fiesta* going on and a knifing a night in the *Barrio*.'

Casteñada's attention was to Lynn O'Hara. 'Did you find your man Ubrecht?'

'I found his room but he's not in it. He's off somewhere. For all we know he could be one of the two men who grabbed a pay satchel last night. If I don't find him today I think I'll take a ride over to

Benson.'

'You'd do better,' Ace Shonsey suggested with a leer, 'to check up on those outlaw cowboys at Old Man Clayton's. You know the way, I understand.'

'Maybe I will,' Lynn said. Beyond that he ignored the gambler and questioned Brokow. 'Do they know which way the payroll robbers went?'

The Tucson marshal nodded. 'Yep, south up the San Pedro. Tracks fade into the river above town. At daybreak they found two silk masks floating down the riffles. Nothing else.'

O'Hara finished his breakfast and hurried to Congress Street. Gary's saloon kept open day and night and the day bartender was now on duty. 'Your man just came in,' he announced when Lynn appeared. He thumbed toward the ceiling. 'Room number five.'

Lynn took the dusty steps two at a time to a dustier hall above. When he knocked at number five he drew a gruff response. 'Yeh? Whatta yuh want?'

'A little conversation, Ubrecht.'

The man who opened the door had a burly, round-shouldered build, a hairy face, disheveled hair, and bloodshot eyes. He looked like a man who'd been up all night in a card game. He'd taken off his coat and outer shirt as though getting ready to catch up on sleep. His gunbelt and holstered gun lay on a bed.

'My name's O'Hara.' Lynn brushed by him and went into the room, where he managed to get between Ubrecht and the bed. It was hard to tell from the man's unshaven, jaded face whether the intrusion puzzled, annoyed, or frightened him. If the name O'Hara alerted him he didn't show it.

'Yeh?'

Lynn sat down on the bed and began making a cigaret. 'You spent the evening of May nineteenth in the Oriental Saloon at Tombstone. You lost all your money in a dice game. According to the Earp brothers, you left right after midnight. Where did you go from there?'

Again Lynn couldn't be sure whether the man was angry or merely puzzled.

His answer came cautiously. 'Can't see as it's any of your business. What's your pitch, mister?'

'You saw my brother leave the saloon with forty-four hundred dollars. At daybreak the twentieth he started by saddle for Tucson. He got as far as the top of the Whetstones and hasn't been seen since. Where were you about that time, Ubrecht?'

Again the man took his time to answer. His eyes fixed on the gun in Lynn's holster and then on his own gun which lay near Lynn on the bed. His retort came guardedly. 'Mindin' my own business.' In a moment he added: 'You're right about me gettin' cleaned out that night. So the next mornin' I went to Charleston to collect a hundred dollars a man there owed me.'

'What's the man's name?'

'Ed Burnett. He runs a meat shop in Charleston. Ed'll tell you I was in Charleston all day the twentieth.'

If true, Ubrecht couldn't have held up Milton O'Hara on top of the Whetstones around midday of the twentieth.

Charleston was on the San Pedro River and only about twelve miles southwest of Tombstone. 'Did you collect the hundred dollars?'

'Sure I did. Used fifty of it to buy a horse and the next day I rode it to Tucson. Been here ever since.'

'Stopped on the way to clean your gun, did you, and shot yourself in the arm?' The arm, after three and a half months was now healed.

'That's right,' Ubrecht made the assertion confidently. 'What's more, I can prove I bought a horse at Charleston on the twentieth. I took a dated bill-of-sale. Want to see it?'

'You bet I would.'

'Here it is. Take a look.' Ben Ubrecht opened a table drawer and his hand rummaged through odds and ends in it. The ruse caught Lynn completely off guard.

For the man's hand came out of the drawer not with a bill-of-sale but with a gun. He aimed it at Lynn's throat. 'Get out of here!' he ordered. 'Get out before I ride you out on a bullet.'

Lynn stood up sheepishly and raised his hands ear high. 'Your drop, Ubrecht. Guess I'll mosey along now; I take it you were kidding about that dated bill-of-sale. You won't mind if I check with the butchershop man Burnett at Charleston?'

'Help yourself. Now get to hell out.'

Assuming the defeated look of a man who knows he's made a wrong guess, Lynn took two steps toward the door.

Then, as he was passing Ubrecht, Lynn whirled and gave a lightning quick slap at the gun the man was pointing at him. His open palm hit the steel of the gun and made it fly from Ubrecht's hand to clatter against a wall of the room.

A breath later the open palm was a clenched fist. Lynn landed it exactly where he'd landed on Shonsey at Madera. On the mouth. He followed with a sweeping swing to the jaw which dropped Ubrecht to the floor.

When Lynn saw he wasn't going to get up he retrieved the gun and took the cartridges from it. Also he took the shells from the gun and gunbelt on the bed. He opened the window and threw the loose cartridges out into the saloon's alley. The empty guns he tossed back on the bed.

Then he looked in the table drawer. To his complete surprise the drawer actually did hold a bill-of-sale for a horse. It was dated at Charleston on May twentieth and signed by Ed Burnett on a letter-head of the Burnett meat shop.

Unless forged it made a fairly firm alibi against any encounter Ubrecht could have had forty miles northwest of Charleston on the Tombstone-to-Tucson stage road.

Feeling much less sure of himself, Lynn doused a pitcher of water over Ubrecht's face and left the room. He must now check with Arturo Casteñada at the courthouse. Had the case against Ubrecht collapsed? Or was it still strong enough to warrant an arrest?

★　★　★

Tucson's new courthouse, not quite finished but with its jail wing already in service, stood just north of Leatherwood's corral and faced the Plaza de las Armas between Pennington and Alameda Streets. Lynn hurried there and at the sheriff's office found only the jailer Jim Lindsay.

'I'm looking for Deputy Casteñada.'

The jailer shrugged. 'Arturo's off around town somewhere. He's digging up witnesses to that gunfight on Meyer Street night before last.'

Lynn waited restlessly for a while. When by late morning Arturo hadn't appeared he went out to look for him. He felt sure that Ubrecht should be arrested and held pending a check on his Charleston alibi for May twentieth.

After crossing the Plaza de las Armas Lynn struck Main Street at the Cosmopolitan Hotel. Teams and freight wagons packed the roadways and lots around it. It was a little bigger and more crowded than the Palace. Strams from a violin orchestra puzzled Lynn. 'Kinda early in the day for music isn't it?'he remarked to a man on the front steps.

'They're rehearsin' for a grand ball tomorrow night.'

Arturo wasn't at the Cosmopolitan nor could Lynn find him on lower Main. At Congress Street he turned west toward Levin's Park in a grove of cottonwoods along a creek. Even this early in the day the grove was active and noisy. Lynn saw tents, booths, a dancing pavilion, open-air dice and faro tables. It was too early for the singing and dancing which would carry on during the afternoon and night.

All around the edges of the grove and for a distance each way along the creek were tents and covered wagons where country Mexicans were camping out for the two weeks of the Feast of San Augustine. Many of these people were already converging upon booths and pavilions where all kinds of food and drink were on sale. Most of the women wore brightly colored skirts and *rebozas* while the men wore serapes, hats with silver bangles, and bell-bottom pantaloons. A few card games were opening up. The main gambling pavilion had set-ups for keno, roulette, monte, and faro. Most of the chatter was in Spanish but Lynn noted a few tough-looking gringos around the game booths.

'A good place to stay away from, O'Hara.' Roger Niles of the *Citizen* came breezily through the crowd. 'You ought to see it at night time. A thousand customers and half of 'em drunk. They tell me it used to be a right decent *fiesta* till the gamblers took over. They used to hold Church Plaza.'

'I'm looking for Arturo. Seen him this morning?'

Niles shook his head. 'But I got a line on your man Ubrecht. I mean I know where he was all day yesterday and last night. He was bucking the tiger right here at this *fiesta*.' The reporter nodded toward a faro table in the main gaming pavilion.

It explained why Ubrecht hadn't shown up at his room till early this morning. Also it proved he couldn't have been one of two men who'd robbed a railroad payroll forty-odd miles to the east.

'You sure of it, Roger?'

'Yep. He and a guy named Chuck Snow from Tombstone spent the day and night tryin' to get rich here. Snow's a bad egg who was tried for a killing at Harshaw in the county court here last March. Got acquitted on what looked like a perjured alibi.'

The name Snow rang a bell in Lynn's memory. He took a list of names from his pocket and saw that one of them was Charley Snow. Wyatt Earp had given him the list at Tombstone. They were the men who'd spent the evening of May nineteenth at the Oriental saloon there.

'Speaking of alibis, Roger, I found Ubrecht this mornin and he offered me one for the day my brother disappeared.'

'Who was he with and where?'

'Said he was at Charleston buying a horse from a man named Burnett.'

'You mean Ed Burnett who runs a meat shop?'

'That's the one. Know anything about

him?'

'Only that he's got a shady rep. He was in court once charged with buying stolen beef from border rustlers. Not enough proof to convict him so he's still in business. The sheriff figures he's in with the Clayton and Curly Max gangs. Buys their stolen beef at half price and butchers it for his shop.'

Lynn's eyes narrowed as he rolled a cigaret. 'Ubrecht's likely in with that crowd. In which case Burnett would be glad to give him a fake bill-of-sale to use for an alibi. Ubrecht who got a bullet through his arm the day my brother disappeared! Two men did that job. If one of them was Ubrecht, the other could be his pal Charley Snow. Let's go find Arturo and talk him into picking them up.'

The yellow-haired reporter gave a brisk nod. 'Lead the way, cowboy. But Arturo'll need help picking up that pair. Especially Chuck Snow. He's poison with a gun.'

# 7

They left the *fiesta* grounds and recrossed Main, entering Congress Street between the Safford bank and the Lord and Williams store. A woman sweeping off the walk in front of the Fashion Theater eyed them curiously. She knew the boyish blond reporter but the tall gunslung cowboy was a stranger. 'Seen Arturo Casteñada this morning?' Roger asked her.

She pointed east up Congress. 'Only a little while ago he comes out of the drugstore and goes that way.'

They walked the length of Congress, past two drugstores, the Lexington livery barn and six saloons. 'I saw him on Maiden Lane fifteen minutes ago,' a man said.

Maiden Lane was a curved street which arced along the north side of the Church Plaza. A few saloons and a row of cheap *bagnios* lined it. Lynn saw jaded, painted faces peering furtively from the crib windows. 'There's an ordinance against it,' Niles said. 'Brokow has to pick 'em up and fine 'em once a month.'

What amazed Lynn O'Hara was that the street inappropriately called Maiden Lane faced a block-square plaza in whose center stood the San Augustine Cathedral. Its brown walls reared with solemn dignity as it stood in stern watch over surrounding lures and evils. Lynn saw a fountain in the churchyard and a priest pacing slowly to and fro, bare tonsured head bowed, hands clasped behind him. In all the wide square plaza he was the only visible life.

'If Arturo is rounding up Mexican witnesses,' Roger Niles suggested, 'he could be in the *Barrio Libre*.' The reporter led Lynn up Court Street to Camp, then east along the south side of the Church Plaza. Here Lynn saw what was clearly a school for young girls. Actually it was a wing of the cathedral itself. A sign announced that it was the convent school of the Sisters of St. Joseph. A nun teacher was shepherding a class of teen-age Spanish girls across a patio.

'Is this the school Don Vicente put his daughter in?'

'Not this year,' Roger said. 'She attended here four or five years, though, between the ages of ten and fifteen. Last year and this year he put her in a gringo school a piece up Convent Street.'

They turned up Convent and presently came to a public park with shade and benches and with a water well at the center. Cartmen were filling water kegs at the well. Across Convent Street from the park Lynn saw a long, two-story building. The lower story was adobe and the upper one was frame. A white picket fence ran in front of it with a narrow strip of hollyhocks and geraniums beyond. From the open upper windows came girlish chatter.

'It's run by a family named Silva,' Roger said. 'The private school where Don Vicente left Gracie yesterday.'

'Gracie?'

'Altagracia Casteñada. Her *Americano*

schoolmates shortened it to Gracie. Look here comes Mike Callahan with another customer.'

A buckboard rolled smartly down Convent Street. The man driving it wore a big cattleman's hat. He looked like a ruddy Irishman and beside him sat a girl with brilliant red hair. She wore a ruffled grey cape with bonnet to match and held a parasol over her head. The man stopped his team at the Silva school carriage block. 'Here we are, Judy. Your last year of schooling and I hope you'll make the most of it.'

The girl laughed merrily. 'I'm planning on having a good time, Papa, if that's what you mean.'

An elderly porter came out to help Mike Callahan unload his daughter's baggage. The girl lifted her wide skirts to step out on the carriage block and from there to the street walk. Then the front door of the school opened and Altagracia Casteñada came dashing out. She raced through the picket gate and into the arms of Judy Callahan.

'They're roommates,' Roger said.

'Older than Gracie, isn't she?' Lynn murmured. 'She's sure a good looker.'

'You mean the redhead? Yeh, she's a year older than Altagracia and being an *Americano* she gets a little longer rope.'

'A longer rope?'

'I mean they're plenty strict here at the Silva school. If a gal goes out to a party it has to be arranged in advance and the escort has to be okayed by the Silvas and the gal's parents. You can't even make a Sunday afternoon call unless a chaperon sits right in the parlor with you.'

Lynn's eyes fixed with a growing fascination on Judy Callahan. 'So you don't think I'd have any luck if I tried getting a date with Miss Redhead?'

'You'd have to start by asking her old man. Then have to ask Miss Silva. Even then you'd get turned down unless you'd known 'em a year. It'd be tougher than that if you tried to date a Spanish girl. Plenty strict on their womenfolks, those *hidalgo* families are.'

Escorted by her father and Altagracia,

95

followed by a porter with her baggage, Judy Callahan disappeared into the school. From its doorway a lean, angular woman looked severely across at two young men on a park bench. 'We better skin out of here,' Lynn said with a grimace, 'before she has us arrested.'

They cut across the park and struck Ochoa Street at Cassel's barn. Just beyond the barn they came to a sordid area about two blocks square, congested with adobe huts, second-rate cantinas, bottle-littered lanes and alleys. Underfed dogs slunk about it. Lynn heard the strumming of a guitar and a chatter in Spanish. Not many were in sight. 'Most of 'em,' Roger Niles said, 'are down at the *fiesta*.'

This was the Free Zone of Tucson — the *Barrio Libre*. A knifing at night! Marshal Ike Brokow had said of this quarter.

The two young men wandered about it on the chance of spotting Arturo. Presently they crossed a narrow lane called Gay Alley, stepped over a sleeping drunk in the Ochoa Street gutter and approached a beer garden. It was next to the big Tully & Ochoa corrals and was shaded by a giant cottonwood. Five men were playing cards in the beer garden. Since entering the *Barrio* every human sighted had been a Latin but these five card players were rough-looking gringos.

All were gunslung and Lynn had seen two of them before. 'Dick Gray and Billy Lang!' he exclaimed guardedly. 'They were hanging out at Old Man Clayton's ranch when I took a haying job there. Wonder what they're doing here at Tucson?'

'And there's Charley Snow!' Roger whispered. 'The guy who spent all day yesterday and last night gambling at the *fiesta* with Ubrecht. And darned if the other two guys aren't . . .'

He took Lynn's arm and led him cautiously out of sight and hearing from the five card players. 'Ever hear of Curly Max?'

'Plenty,' Lynn said. 'They say he heads a gang of border thieves. Sometimes they hang out at Charleston and sometimes at Galeyville. I hear they've got a feud on with the Earp crowd at Tombstone. You tellin' me one of those guys is Curly Max?'

'No. But all five of them ride with him. They raid with him, take orders from him. That 'n with the flat, black hat is Frankie Byers. Other four are Dick Gray, Billy Lang, Lew Pardee, and Charley Snow. Every one of 'em has faced a murder charge in the county court here, at one time or another. They always get off — either with a rigged alibi or a self-defense plea supported by perjured witnesses.' Roger Niles peered over an adobe wall at the card players. They sat coatless, perspiring in the sultry heat, each with a mug of beer by him. 'A mean bunch, those five! Ever hear of the Fronteras massacre, across the border in Sonora?'

Lynn nodded. 'They say twenty gringo cowboys waylaid sixteen Mexican traders. Fired into 'em from ambush, killed six, scattered the rest and got away with four thousand in cash.'

'That's it. And the leading suspects are the five gunnies you're looking at right now — plus Curly Max himself and the Clayton crew. Let's get out of here before they spot us.'

It was time to eat and they headed for the Palace Hotel. 'What,' Lynn puzzled, 'would those five rowdies be doing here at the county seat?'

Roger was equally puzzled. 'First time I ever knew 'em to come except when they're brought here to stand trial for some devilment. But you can bet they've got a reason. I'd sure like to know where they were at midnight last night, when a payroll was snatched at Benson.'

'We know where Charley Snow was. He was gambling at the Tucson *fiesta* with Ubrecht.'

'It still leaves four of 'em,' Roger brooded, 'for the job at Benson. But you'd think they'd take off to one of their mountain hideouts with the money, 'stead of riding straight to Tucson with it.'

'Dollars to doughnuts,' Lynn guessed, 'that Ubrecht'll join 'em soon as he catches up on sleep.'

After lunch they went again to the courthouse hoping to find Arturo. 'You just missed him,' the jailer said. 'He rode out to Fort Lowell. Said he'd be back by nightfall. Couple of soldiers were on Meyer Street night before last and they could've seen that shoot-out. Arturo wants to tap 'em as witnesses.'

It was eight miles to Fort Lowell. Lynn put in a restless afternoon waiting for Arturo's return. Twice during it he strolled into the *Barrfo Libre* to see if five outlaws were still in the beer garden. They were still there at sundown. Lynn kept wondering what they were up to. Tucson was the seat of county law and the Curly Max gang usually operated at least a day's ride away from it.

Right now they'd know that the sheriff's crew, except for one young deputy, was far away on a chase after horse thieves. Were the five planning some bold raid right here in town?

Just before nightfall Arturo Casteñada appeared and Lynn met him at the Palace Hotel hitchrail. 'I cannot imagine why they are here,' he said when Lynn told him about the five men.

Next Lynn told of his encounter with Ubrecht in the man's room over Gary's bar. 'What about picking him up?'

Arturo shrugged and shook his head. 'You were wrong to accuse him without proof, my friend. He had a right to order you from his room. A court would say that you were the aggressor for intruding there and striking him.'

'Then there's no case against him?'

'Not enough for an arrest. Let us go to the Maison Dorée for a glass of wine and we will talk it over.'

At a French restaurant on Meyer Street they had not only a glass of wine but supper. It was dark when they left the place. 'Does this Ubrecht have a police record here?' Lynn asked.

'If so it is nothing serious. Let us go and see.'

At the sheriff's office they checked the

records and found that no county charge had ever been lodged against Ben Ubrecht. But when they crossed an alley to the city jail and asked Marshal Ike Brokow, Brokow remembered a drunk and disorderly charge once placed against Ubrecht. 'It was two or three months ago. We kept him overnight in jail and then turned him loose.'

A check of the books showed that it had occurred on May twenty-ninth, just a week after Ubrecht had arrived in town with a bullet-nicked arm. Then Arturo remembered a routine of police procedure whenever a prisoner is jailed. 'You take his pocket articles and give him a receipt. You return them when he is released. What pocket articles did Ubrecht have that night?'

The answer was found in the jail records.

'*Caramba!*' exclaimed Arturo when he saw the list of pocket articles which Ubrecht had carried on May twenty-ninth. One of the items was a wallet containing twenty-one hundred dollars in currency.

Lynn's eyes took a shrewd gleam. 'It fits Arturo. If he and another man took forty-four hundred dollars from my brother, Ubrecht's cut would be half of it. He'd spend about a hundred of it during a week here in Tucson. Which'd leave him about twenty-one hundred. Remember he was dead broke when he left Tombstone.'

'It makes reason,' Arturo agreed. 'Now we have ground to arrest him. Let us go do so at once.'

They hurried to Gary's saloon. 'Is Ubrecht in his room?' Arturo asked the barman.

The barman shrugged. '*Quien sabe?* Ain't seen him since early morning.'

Lynn and Arturo went upstairs and found room number five deserted. Every scrap of Ben Ubrecht's baggage was gone. There were back stairs which the man could have used to avoid paying his room bill.

'He must have pulled out,' Arturo concluded, 'right after you were here this morning. Your suspicions frightened him and so he has been riding all day. Now he will have all night to hide his tracks.'

His tracks to where?, Lynn wondered. To a partner in crime who'd helped him hold up and rob Milton O'Hara? It had to be a two-man Job. The companion had cut a sleeve from his own white linen shirt to make a bandage for Ubrecht's arm. And Ubrecht had arrived here not with all nor with a third or fourth, but with *half* of the stolen money.'

Somewhere in this desert county another man had the other half. Was Ubrecht now riding to warn him? Or to be hidden by him? A grimness lined Lynn's face. 'I'm going after them, Arturo. If it takes the rest of my life I've got to run them down.'

# 8

'When will Sheriff Shibell get back?' Lynn asked when they went out to the street.

'He should arrive from the border tomorrow,' Arturo answered. 'But tonight on the train from Florence another sheriff will come. Our good friend Sheriff Pete Gabriel of Pinal County. I must meet his train at half past ten. Then I must see him off again at five in the morning. I envy you a full night's sleep, *amigo. Buenas noches.*'

Arturo turned toward the courthouse and Lynn walked toward the Palace Hotel. Half absently he wondered why the young deputy would meet a visiting sheriff at one train and see him off on another, the same night. The eastbound due through Tucson at ten-thirty would be the train which would arrive at Benson at midnight, and which last night had carried an unlucky paymaster. From

Benson it would continue on to end-of-track at Wilcox. From Wilcox it would return west and pass through Tucson at five in the morning.

A little odd, though, that a visiting sheriff couldn't arrive on the eastbound and leave six and a half hours later on the west-bound without keeping Arturo up all night to see him arrive and depart.

Lynn was about to turn in at the Palace when he decided to have one more look at the Ochoa Street beer garden. Were the five border outlaws still there? What were they up to? Were they waiting for someone and could that someone be Ubrecht? Ubrecht who'd spent all day yesterday and last night with Charley Snow at the *fiesta*! There was no certainty that Ubrecht had left town this morning. He might be hiding in one of the *Barrio* dives and planning to leave under cover of darkness.

Lynn continued on up Meyer to Ochoa and stopped in the black shadow of a cottonwood tree which cornered the beer garden. The cantina serving the garden was noisy with clapping and song. Lynn heard a guitar and the clack of castanets.

The garden itself was empty except for a table occupied by the five Curly Max raiders. Lynn remembered their names — Dick Gray, Billy Lang, Charley Snow, Lew Pardee and Frank Byers. They weren't drinking now. Three of them were eating tortillas and the other two were dozing. It struck Lynn that they were killing time, perhaps waiting for someone or for some specific hour of action.

Any one of them could be the man who'd helped Ubrecht rob Milton O'Hara. Any one of them could have in his wallet right now the unspent part of the second twenty-two hundred dollars! A savage impulse to stick with them and find out gripped Lynn.

He walked around the outside of a high adobe wall until he got opposite them. What were they talking about? Maybe they'd mention Ubrecht. Or perhaps mention some hide-out or rendezvous to which Ubrecht might at this moment be riding.

Lynn caught only a few snatches of talk.

'You grained the broncs, did you, Lew?' The question was Charley Snow's as he thumbed over his shoulder to a row of tethered horses just outside the rear wall. The animals weren't saddled but a saddle for each of them was draped over the wall.

Pardee grunted an affirmative. 'We better get some shut eye, Chuck. In just eight hours we gotta fan the breeze.'

In a few minutes all five men were stretched back in their chairs, dozing. Why, Lynn wondered, didn't they go to rooming house and rent cots? Why weren't their mounts stalled in a livery barn? Lynn counted the horses and there were six.

Six horses for five men! It meant that another man was expected to join them. Could he be Ubrecht?

If so, why would they delay eight hours before riding out of town? Since it was only nine in the evening, eight hours from now would be five in the morning.

*If Ubrecht shows up, can't take him away from them. They'd be six to one and they'd gun me down.* Lynn walked back down Meyer Street and again he passed his hotel without stopping. The situation called for a conference with Arturo. Maybe they could enlist a few of Ike Brokow's town constables and go in force to pick up Ubrecht when and if he appeared at the beer garden.

At the sheriff's office Arturo listened to him impassively until a certain phrase made him suddenly alert. '*Eight hours!*' he exclaimed. 'Are you sure they said eight hours from now?

'That's right. In just eight hours they'll be fanning the breeze. Where to they didn't say.'

Arturo's dark Latin eyes narrowed. 'And you think the extra horse is for Ubrecht?'

'Who else?'

'Come, I will show you. You have made a great discovery, Lynn, but it is different from the way you think.' In a growing excitement Arturo led Lynn into a jail corridor and to a cell which held a single hard-eyed prisoner. The man stared sullenly through the bars at them.

'His name,' Arturo explained, 'is Gil Stilwell. A month ago he holds up a stagecoach in Pinal County, north of here and kills a Wells Fargo messenger. A week ago we pick him up here in Tucson. We notify the Pinal County Sherif, Pete Gabriel, who comes for him on tonight's train. On the next train west, which passes through at five in the morning Sheriff Pete will take his prisoner back to Florence. Where, because his crimes were well witnessed, he is sure to be found guilty and hanged.'

Lynn clamped his wits on it. Two things were due to happen at five in the morning. A sheriff would board a train at the Tucson depot with a hand-cuffed prisoner; and five border outlaws, having brought along an extra horse, were planning to 'fan the breez.'

'Leaves only one question,' Lynn said grimly. 'Are they pals — the Curly Max gang and Stilwell?'

'*Compadres* in many a raid, Arturo confirmed. Often he has been seen with them in the saloons of Galeyville and Charleston. And like Curly Max and the Claytons, Gil Stilwell has a blood feud with the Earp brothers at Tombstone.'

'So it's a rescue play!' Lynn concluded. 'They know Shibell's away and nobody here but you. They figure you'll escort Gabriel and his prisoner from Jail to the train, just before daybreak. In the dark they gun you down and ride away fast with Stilwell.'

Arturo shrugged an assent, then gave a sly smile. 'But I shall fool them, Lynn O'Hara. Now that you have brought me this warning, I shall recommend to Pete Gabriel that he lay over a day. Shibell will be back tomorrow and there will be many to guard when we take the prisoner to a train tomorrow night.'

'Suppose Gabriel is stubborn and insists on going tonight?

'He is a wise man and discreet,' Arturo argued, and he will not take such a chance. But just to play safe I shall ask Marshal Brokow to lend me his night force of policemen. We shall guard the jail well till Señor Shibell returns from the border.'

Lynn said a dubious goodnight and walked to his room at the Palace. There he went to bed and tried to sleep. At half past ten he heard the whistle of a train as it came in from the west and rumbled to a stop at the depot.

The Pinal County sheriff would be getting off that train.

Arturo would meet and warn him; then they'd go to the jail and talk things over with Ike Brokow. Would they run the gauntlet of five outlaw killers waiting to rescue Stilwell somewhere between the jail and the depot? Or would they take Arturo's advice and hold Stilwell in Tucson for a day or two longer? It seemed to Lynn that the sensible thing would be to wait at least until the return of Sheriff Shibell.

Presently Lynn fell into a disturbed and restless sleep. He wakened in the dark, struck a match and looked at his watch. It was four o'clock — just an hour before a westbound train was due. What decision had been made at the jail? Presumably the five renegades at the Ochoa Street beer garden didn't know they were suspected of planning a rescue. About now they'd be moving into position near the depot, ready to strike, snatch a prisoner from Gabriel and speed away by saddle.

The possibilities and uncertainties nagged at Lynn. He got up, dressed, buckled on his gunbelt, and went out to the street. The Meyer Street saloons were still lighted as he walked south toward Ochoa. As he neared the *Barrio* the street became darker and dingier. He came to a cottonwood-shaded beer garden with a high adobe wall around it.

Looking over the wall he failed to see the five gringos from Galeyville. A hitchrail where their six horses had been tied was now empty.

It convinced Lynn that they'd ridden to the vicinity of the Southern Pacific depot. There they could hide behind boxcars on a siding while waiting for Gabriel and a prisoner. City Marshall Brokow had no doubt scouted the situation by now and would govern himself accordingly.

To make sure, and to lend a hand himself, Lynn hurried down Court Street to the courthouse jail. There he found six heavily armed lawmen — Marshal Brokaw, three of his policemen, Deputy Sheriff Arturo Casteñada and a sheriff from a neighboring county who'd arrived at half past ten. The jailer had just brought a hand-cuffed prisoner from his cell.

In the street in front stood a two-horse hack. Four saddled horses were tied at the same rack. Apparently the plan was to wait till a few minutes before train time and then make a dash under guard for the depot.

'They'll be laying for you!' Lynn warned.

Brokow gave a curt nod. 'We know it. I scouted 'em myself. Half an hour ago they moved from the beer garden to the tracks. Tied their broncs back of the freight house. Right now they're eating chop suey at a Chinese joint on Toole Street, across from the depot.' The marshal had a short-barreled shotgun under his arm and a forty-five at his belt.

Arturo took a repeating rifle from the riot gun rack. His lean, Latin face had distress on it. The look on the broad, bearded face of Sheriff Pete Gabriel was grimly stubborn.

'They will not take my advice' Arturo said to Lynn 'and wait till Shibell returns from the border.'

'It's none of my business,' Lynn offered, 'but seems to me the smart thing'd be to swear in about a dozen deputies and surround that chop suey joint. Glad to help out, if you want me. We could arrest those five bums and lock 'em up till Sheriff Gabriel gets his man on the train.'

'Arrest 'em for what?' Brokow protested. 'They haven't done anything yet. We're only guessing they plan a rescue. You can't arrest 'em for stayin' up all night and orderin' a bowl of chop suey.'

'They'll be shooting from cover,' Lynn predicted, 'when you get to the depot. Shooting from boxcars and dark alleys. They can cut you to pieces before you know where they are.' He remembered what he'd heard about an ambush near Fronteras, across the border. These same outlaw cowboys along with others of their stripe had fired into a group of peaceful Mexican traders, killing six in cold blood. Tonight they'd hardly hesitate to do the same when a hack passed them in the dark, near the depot.

'But we'll fool 'em,' Pete Gabriel said with a grim smile, 'and board the train not at the depot but at the Rillito water tank, five miles down the track. Let's get started, boys. Glad to have you come along, O'Hara, if you feel like it.'

With a sense of intense relief Lynn went out to the hack with them. This, he admitted, was the right solution. To bypass the ambush. A direct route to the Rillito Creek water tank would miss the depot by eight blocks. The would-be rescuers would be left holding a bag, like cheated snipe hunters.

'Count me in, Sheriff,' Lynn agreed cheerfully. 'Where do you want me to ride?'

'Take your choice,' the Pinal County man said. 'Inside with me or up front with the driver.'

A blocky constable named Buttner climbed to the driver's seat and took the reins. His shotgun was of the type carried by Wells Fargo messengers. Lynn, armed only with a holster gun, took the seat by him. Gabriel shoved his prisoner into the hack and got in himself. The other two policemen, along with Brokow and Casteñada, stepped into saddles. 'Let's roll,' Brokow said.

The hack with its four outriders moved down Alameda Street to Main and northerly out Main on a trail which, until the recent arrival of rail service, had been a stage coach route to Florence, Yuma, and California. 'Take us nearly an hour to get there,' Constable Buttner estimated. 'We can just make it.'

'We'll flag the train?' Lynn asked him.

'Won't need to. It's a regular water stop.'

They passed the last Main Street cantina and beyond the only light was from moon and stars. Buttner whipped his team and they made dust along the wheel-cut ruts with the four outriders keeping abreast. Inside the hack Pete Gabriel sat with his manacled prisoner.

For minutes there were only hoof and wheel sounds. Then Lynn heard a chuckle from Arturo. 'I would like to see their faces, *amigos*, when the train comes and we do not arrive at the depot.'

'We sure gave 'em the slip' Buttner agreed. 'Time they find out we're not gonna show up it'll be too late.' He kept his team at a smart trot down the *camino real*.

A six-span mule team from Casa Grande, travelling at night to avoid the desert heat, met and passed them.

Then Buttner turned his hack off on a side trail which would strike the Southern Pacific track at a water tank on the bank of Rillito Creek. Lynn looked at his watch. It was three minutes before five o'clock and far back of him, to the east, a train whistled. 'There she is,' Brokow called from his saddle. 'In a few minutes she'll pull up at the depot. Those guys'll sure look stupid when we don't show up with Stilwell.'

Off up Rillito Creek, in the direction of Fort Lowell a coyote yapped. Then Lynn thought he heard another sound perhaps a mile behind him on the road. Was it a drum of hoofbeats? Were they being followed?

Stupid, Brokow called those fellows. But were they? Wouldn't they be smart enough to do a little scouting themselves? Might not one of them have been sent to the courthouse jail to check on whether or not the lawmen were coming?

Such a scout would have seen the hack's departure with outriders for a down-track tank. He'd lose no time in reporting to the others. Again Lynn thought he heard pursuing hoofbeats. 'Sounds like they're gaining on us,' he said to Buttner.

The shape of a water tank came in sight and presently the hack pulled up beside it. On the spout side of the tank ran the railroad track and beyond the track a few scrub cottonwoods lined the bank of Rillito Creek.

As Lynn jumped to the ground Sheriff Pete Gabriel was prodding his prisoner out of the hack. 'Listen, Sheriff! We're about to have company.'

By now all the lawmen had heard the hoof sounds. *'Caramba!'* exclaimed Arturo Casteñada.

There was a tension of quiet while they listened to approaching horsemen. 'Let 'em come!' Ike Brokow said grimly. 'We'll be ready for 'em.'

As the senior local officer he took charge and posted his men. 'Shepherd, you and Buttner take the prisoner and the horses and get in the creek bed. Arturo, you and O'Reilly take cover in those rocks. Pete, you and I and O'Hara'll stand under the tank. They won't see us in the shadow there.'

Quickly the defenders were in position. Lynn, standing between Gabriel and Brokow under a dripping cypress tank, drew his forty-five and waited. A cold anger filled him when he remembered that one of the oncomers was Charley Snow, a crony of Ubrecht's; which meant that Snow might well be the man who'd helped Ubrecht rob and murder Milton O'Hara. Or any one of the five oncoming outlaws could have been with Ubrecht that day.

The sound of horsemen came nearer. 'It's them, all right,' Brokow whispered. He had a shotgun and Gabriel carried a repeating rifle. 'I'll give 'em a chance to throw down their guns. If they don't, we blast 'em.'

Gabriel nodded. 'Just like they blasted those sixteen Mexicans at Fronteras.'

Somewhere out in the darkness the oncomers stopped. Lynn sensed that they were dismounting to maneuver. Their best tactic would be to creep up from five directions. Probably they didn't know they were outnumbered seven to five. All horses except the hack team were now out of sight in the creek bed.

The next minutes were soundless. Then faintly from a far distance to the east the desert night brought to Lynn two quick, short toots. Two toots from an engine at the Tucson depot, as a west-bound train made ready to pull out.

Then abruptly Lynn heard gunshots from the creek bed. They were followed by shouts and more gunshots. The voice of Buttner came hoarsely: 'This way, Ike; Pete; in the creek.'

Pete Gabriel dashed out from under the tank, crossed the track and lost himself in the shadow of a creekbank cottonwood. Brokow and O'Hara were only a step behind him. Gunfire was flashing from three spots in the nearly dry creek bed. Two outlaws were down-creek and three were upcreek, all five of them shooting it out with Buttner and Shepherd. The hand-cuffed prisoner had thrown himself flat on his face.

Lynn drew and sent five bullets toward the three men upcreek. They were no more than dim silhouettes. Brokow with his shotgun and Gabriel with a rifle were pouring lead downcreek.

Two of the upcreek trio fell; the other turned and ran. He ran straight into Constable O'Reilly who smashed a charge of buckshot into his stomach. From downcreek came more crackling shots, then a yell from Arturo Casteñada. '*Son muertos, las dos!*' They are dead; both of them!

Lynn could hardly believe it was over so swiftly. He holstered his gun and went to make sure of it. He found Arturo and O'Reilly standing by Billy Lang and Frankie Byers; both of them were full of bullets and past breathing.

Upcreek there was one survivor — Lew Pardee. Charley Snow and Dick Gray were riddled and dead. Pardee, by some miracle, had only a slight leg wound. 'They had it coming,' Brokow said. None of his own force was even scratched. Arturo's thin face twitched in the starlight. 'What happened to them,' he said, 'is what happened to my countrymen at Fronteras. The *sin verguenzas*!'

Brokow swabbed his forehead to wipe away sweat. 'We'll load em in the hack, boys, and take 'em to town.'

'All but one,' Pete Gabriel corrected. He jerked a grovelling prisoner to his feet. 'You and I, Gil Stilwell, are boarding a train for Florence. And here she comes.'

The California-bound Southern Pacific train five miles out of Tucson, came pounding to a stop at the Rillito tank. While a fireman swung the spout over a tender, Gabriel hustled his man aboard. 'Thanks, boys,' he called back.

Lynn O Hara, with five Tucson lawmen, stood by the track and watched the train move out and fade into the desert darkness.

# 9

Through the morning hours Lynn slept soundly in his room at the Palace. It was nearly noon when he got down to the courthouse and found that Sheriff Charles Shibell and a saddle-weary posse had just returned from a chase into Mexico. They had recovered four stolen horses and on the way back had dropped them at Calabasas. But the killers of Panacho Morales were still uncaught. 'We muffed it,' Shibell admitted dourly as he kicked boots from his swollen feet. We rode the skin off our saddles and we've got nothing but blisters to show for it.'

'And while you were away,' Ike Brokow added with a grimace, 'couple of guys knocked over a payroll at Benson.'

'But last night,' Arturo Casteñada put in by way of consolation, 'we had better luck. Of five shameless ones who try to rob us of a prisoner, four are in the morgue and one is in Jail.' He looked at Lynn O'Hara who had just come in. 'We owe it to our friend from Wyoming who warned us of the plot.'

The sheriff gave a gruff greeting. 'Hello there, O'Hara. Met you at Madera on my way south. You were figuring to look up a man named Ubrecht. Didja find him?'

Lynn nodded. 'But he skipped town before I could get anything on him. I'm sure now he's one of the two men who waylaid my brother.'

'Chances are,' Shibell reasoned, 'that he's hiding out with any one of a dozen shoestring ranchers between here and New Mexico. Crooked ranchers, I mean. Some of 'em take out homestead claims for a front. Some just move into an abandoned cabin and call it a ranch. Generally it's just a raiding base. Nearly all of 'em take orders from Curly Max or Old Man Clayton.' He elevated his sock feet to a desk and the swivel chair creaked as he leaned his bulk back in it. 'Criminy, I'm bushed! Somebody fetch me a sandwich and a mug of beer.'

The refreshment revived him and as soon as he had the situation in hand he began passing out orders. 'Juho,' he directed his undersheriff, 'grab some sleep and then catch the night train to Benson. Get busy on the payroll robbery and stick with it.' Turning to his next ranking deputies, Rudolph Gorman and Jim Evarts, he instructed them to follow up on the casualties of last night's gunfight at a water tank. 'You've got four dead men, a leg-shot prisoner and six horses. Process and evaluate everything on 'em.'

'It has already been done,' Arturo Casteñada told him. 'One of the dead men has an uncashed pay check from the Clayton ranch. Not much on the others except a little money and cartridges and some beer checks issued by the saloons of Tombstone and Charleston. Two of the horses, by the brands, were stolen from the Sierra Boruta ranch of Señor Hooker near Camp Grant.'

'Go through everything again,' Shibell

insisted. 'Turn every pocket and saddle-bag inside out. Soon as I get some sleep I'll take a hand myself. And don't forget, all of you who were at the water tank fight will have to testify at the inquests tomorrow.'

Lynn left them and went to the Lexington livery barn for a look at his horse. The roan had been well cared for and the barn crew bombarded Lynn with questions about the water tank gunfight. He was waylaid a dozen more times on the street.

On this Thursday morning, the second day of September, the town was boiling with excitement. As though the truth weren't enough, weird exaggerations had been built on top of it. Curly Max himself, the street crowds were saying, had led the rescue attempt and was now in the morgue along with such of his stalwart *segundos* as Zwing Hunter and Johnnie Ringo. Another version was that the four Earp brothers, along with Doc Holliday, had come up from Tombstone to take part in exterminating five of their enemies.

Three times along Congress Street Lynn had to strip these fabrications down to their proper dimensions. Then he spotted the bare, yellow-haired head of a *Citizen* reporter on the walk in front of Gary's bar.

'Let's take another look at Ubrecht's room,' Lynn suggested.

Roger Niles went into Gary's with him. Room number five was still empty and the barman let them go up there. Nobody was saying no to Lynn O'Hara today. Somehow he had emerged as the hero of last night's water tank fight because word was out that it was he who'd first discovered the rescue plan and had warned the lawmen of it.

Room number five hadn't even been swept out. 'Let's go over it again, Rog, in case I overlooked something.'

Roger Niles went through a waste basket and took an old newspaper from it. It was a month-old copy of the Tombstone *Epitaph*. The name and address of the subscriber to whom it had been mailed was printed on it.

Joe Dawson
Contention City, A.T.

Lynn asked, 'Is Dawson another name Ubrecht has used?' 'No,' Roger told him. 'Dawson's a guy they call Durango Joe. He's got a shack and a fenced quarter section on the San Pedro between Contention City and Benson. Gets his mail at Contention. Used to run with the Clayton-Curly Max bunch, they say. He was tried for a killing last winter but was acquitted.'

'Self defense plea?'

'Not that. Wait a minutes. Let me think. I covered the trial myself.' Niles knitted his brow and concentrated. 'I remember. A witness turned up and swore him a cast iron alibi. And come to think of it, the witness was Ben Ubrecht.'

It was Roger's opinion that the alibi testimony had been bald perjury. But since no one could refute it, it had saved Joe Dawson's neck.

'So they're pards, Dawson and Ubrecht,' Lynn concluded. 'Looks like

130

Ubrecht stopped at Dawson's cabin about a month ago and picked up this Tombstone paper.'

'Either that,' Roger Niles agreed, 'or else something of mutual interest in it made Dawson mail it to Ubrecht here at Tucson. Let's take a look.'

They spread the month-old copy of the *Epitaph* out and went through all of its six pages. One short item was marked with a circle.

Wyatt Earp has been appointed deputy county sheriff at Tombstone by Sheriff Shibell at Tucson.

'Why,' Lynn wondered, 'would it interest Dawson and Ubrecht?'

'That's easy,' Roger explained. 'There's a feud between the Curly Max clique of crooked cowboys and the Earp brothers at Tombstone. Everybody thinks it's just a question of time until it ends up in one bang-up shoot-out. Now this deputyship of Wyatt Earp gives him a badge to back up his gun. Makes it harder for the cowboy clique to deal with him.'

Lynn caught the idea. 'I see. So Durango Joe, under obligation to Ubrecht for a courtroom alibi, warns Ubrecht by mailing him a copy of the *Epitaph* which reports the appointment.'

'Not that it's any help to us,' Roger said as they left the room, 'in finding out where Ubrecht skeedaddled to.'

'On the other hand,' Lynn argued, 'maybe it's just the tip we need. Ubrecht took off for an unknown hideout. Why wouldn't it be the cabin of his friend Joe on the San Pedro? He saved Joe's neck with a phony alibi; so the least Joe can do is to hide him for a while; or maybe pack grub to him at some shack in the hills till I quit hunting for him.'

'Makes sense, Lynn. You going to check it out?'

'I sure am. Have to show up at some inquests tomorrow. Soon as I'm through here in town I'll head for the San Pedro and see what I can turn up at Durango Joe's.'

'If you turn up Ubrecht,' the reporter

warned, 'he'll have Joe Dawson siding him. So you'd better take someone along with you.'

In the afternoon Lynn took it up with Sheriff Shibell. The sheriff spread his hands helplessly. 'Wish I could spare somebody. But I can't. Things are stacked up here on us. Half my crew'll be working on the Benson payroll robbery. And we still haven't caught up with whoever killed Pancho Morales at Calabasas.'

'Why,' Lynn argued, 'is one murder case more important than another?'

'It's not. But we can't classify your brother's case as murder. No corpus delicti. On the books it's just a mysterious disappearance.'

'He was murdered for forty-four hundred dollars,' Lynn insisted. 'Next day Ubrecht showed up at Doctor Handy's office with half the money and a bullet-pinked arm. Three and a half months later he finds I'm on his tail so he slips out of town.'

Shibell frowned over it for a minute. 'Tell you what, O'Hara. I can't spare a deputy to help you right now. But I can give you some authority. If you'll accept a temporary deputyship you can have it. Fact is you earned it in that water tank shoot-out last night.'

'It might help,' Lynn admitted. He raised his right hand. 'Swear me in, Sheriff.'

A badge was on his jacket when he left the office.

Walking down Pennington he struck Main at the Cosmopolitan Hotel and stopped at the bar there for a beer. In a big dining room off the lobby festive preparations were under way for a ball tomorrow night. The lobby was full of chatter about it and a committee of ladies were putting up decorations.

As he went out Lynn ran into Arturo Casteñada. 'I reckon you'll be here, Arturo, you being one of the old families.'

'But of course. All the world of importance will be here. Which must include you, my friend. I will present you to some beautiful ladies.'

'One of them,' Lynn ventured, 'would be that cute little cousin of yours?'

The suggestion mildly shocked Arturo. 'Altagracia? But no, *amigo*. It would not be permitted.' With a faint smile he added: 'Our friend Roger Niles has spoken to Miss Silva on the matter. He would like very much to dance a quadrille with Gracia. But they have told him it is impossible. Only after my cousin is married or betrothed will she be allowed to attend a public dance.'

'Seems like that's ridin' kinda close herd on her,' Lynn said. 'You'd think they'd let her have a little fun, once in a while. Well, have a good time yourself, Arturo.'

Lynn left him and spent the rest of the day meandering about downtown Tucson and the district called the *Barrio Libre*. In the evening he circled the *fiesta* grounds, keeping his eyes open, just in case he'd guessed wrong about Ben Ubrecht leaving town. Nowhere did he catch a glimpse of the man.

Just before bedtime, however, he

spotted another enemy — the gambler Ace Shonsey. Shonsey had rigged himself in a new checkered suit and bright yellow boots. He was flushed with whisky as he stood at a Maiden Lane bar. Again a bulge at his left breast indicated an armpit holster. Lynn, remembering a thirty-eight the man had pulled on him at a stage station, didn't accost him.

Instead he went to his room at the Palace and to bed.

★ ★ ★

On Friday, September third the life of Tucson flowed in three mainstreams of activity. There was the normal routine of saloon, restaurant and street life, with faro banks operating at the Fashion Bar, at Brown's Congress Hall and at the Frenchman Paul Abadie's popular saloon on Meyer Street; as well as the singing and clack of chips at the big gambling picnic called the Feast of San Augustine and the rabber carousals in the *Barrio*. Then there was the police life of both city and county forces, on constant patrol of the streets, and at the courthouse a series of coroner's inquests at which all who'd taken part in the water tank gunfight had to testify. These kept Lynn O'Hara in attendance until it was too late to begin a forty-five mile ride to the San Pedro.

He ordered his roan to be grained for an early start Saturday morning. The third stream of movement began flowing late Friday afternoon. Formally uniformed officers from Fort Lowell, some with their ladies, began coming in by saddle and carriage to register at the Palace and Cosmopolitan hotels. Ranch couples in their party best drove in from up and down the Santa Cruz River, from valleys in the Rincons and Santa Catalinas, and by train from as far away as Florence and Casa Grande. The oldest families of Tucson, like the Ochoas and the Ourys and the Saffords, opened their fine houses on South Main to take in overnight guests.

The best orchestra in the Arizona

Territory was tuned up and ready for the dancing which would begin at nine o'clock.

As dusk fell over the town the carriages began rolling, all converging on the Cosmopolitan. Lynn stood at the Zechendorf corner on the *camino real* and watched them pass. Army officers in gold braid, the single ones on their cavalry mounts, the married ones in carriages with gayly gowned wives and daughters. The best of Tucson was on parade tonight and a lonely Wyoming cowboy suddenly felt an itch to be part of it. He might look in for a while, mightn't he, even if he didn't dance?

★ ★ ★

A few blocks south and east, up Convent Street, a far more poignant wistfulness to be part of it assailed some thirty-odd young lady boarders at the Silva school. Most of them were too young to properly attend a hotel dance. A few were town girls whose *Americano* parents had already called for them and would chaperon them to the ball. Of those who were from distant ranches, or from distant cities like Phoenix or Prescott, only one had been given permission to be called for by a male escort. This one was an eighteen-year-old girl with lovely fair skin and bright red hair — the pampered daughter of Mike Callahan whose Circle C ranch was on Cienega Creek, twenty-five miles east of town.

It left more than two dozen of the girls who couldn't go at all. Nothing was left for them except the vicarious thrill of helping to get Judy Callahan ready for the party. All afternoon they'd been at it, rejoicing with her, envying her, advising her, admiring her, showering her with excited questions about the man who would call in a carriage at nine.

None was more excited than Judy's roommate, Altagracia Casteñada. How boldly unconventional these American parents were, she thought, to allow a girl to go out at night with a man even before she was engaged to marry him! Down in

Sonora, among gentlefolk, it was never done.

Darkness came to Convent Street and with it the magic hour of nine. Altagracia helped Judy on with her cape. 'He will think you are beautiful,' she predicted.

'Let's hope so,' the ranch girl said brightly. 'Don't wait up for me, Gracie.'

The escort's carriage had already stopped in front. As Judy went downstairs, Altagracia blew out the lamp and rushed to the room's street window. From it she could see a closed carriage with a coachman on the box. Coming through the picket gate was a tall, slender man, gloved and hatted, a party cape loosely over his shoulders. No gangling schoolboy this, but a mature gentleman of the world. Twenty-five years old, according to Judy. Judy had admitted too that he was in high favor with her father and had once helped Mike Callahan stand off some raiding Apaches. Altagracia knew that Mike Callahan was of a school who believed that a girl should be safely married by the time she was twenty. It made everything seem so final. Who could doubt but that Judy, soon after this school term, would become the bride of the man to whom she was being entrusted tonight? The prospect lent an extra thrill to the occasion.

A brass knocker down below sounded and then the door was opened by Miss Silva herself. There were murmured greetings which Altagracia couldn't hear. She knew that many of the other young girls were watching from their own windows.

Then three people emerged from the entrance and moved down the walk, through the picket gate and to the carriage block in front. They were Judy Callahan, her tall escort, and the watchful Miss Silva. Gracia saw the escort hand Judy into the carriage. She heard a final admonition from Miss Silva. 'The permission was granted, you understand, only on the condition that you have her home by midnight.'

The man took off his hat, bowed a goodnight to Miss Silva. 'That'll be about three hours before the party breaks up. But anything you say, ma'am.'

He got into the carriage. The coachman snapped his whip and the carriage rolled away.

At her window Altagracia stood breathless. When the escort had taken off his hat to say goodnight, she'd had a good look at his face. Moonlight and the door lamp had revealed it clearly. It was a face she'd seen before from another upper window — a hotel window at Calabasas.

The face of a thief who'd helped to steal four horses and who'd shot a bullet through Pancho Morales!

# 10

The grand ball at the Cosmopolitan wasn't an invitation affair. Tickets were five dollars a couple or three dollars for a single admission, the proceeds being tagged for the welfare of Papago Indian orphans.

Lynn O'Hara shaved and put on a fresh shirt. He polished his boots, took off his spurs and gun. They'd told him guns were forbidden on the dance floor except when worn by law officers on duty. Lynn had a deputy badge but he decided not to take advantage of it. He left the badge with his gun and spurs and walked briskly from the Palace on Meyer Street to the Cosmopolitan on lower Main.

Before buying a ticket he looked in from the ballroom's doorway. All the women were in lowcut finery and were matched in formality by a score of officers from the fort. Many of the civilian males present wore broadcloth and starched shirts. Yet Lynn saw many who didn't. Ranchers and cattle hands were there, milling about with the others, and these were rigged out much as was Lynn himself. He spotted the veteran stockman Pete Kitchen, whose only concession to convention had been to put on a black church suit and a string tie.

The third number of the evening, a quadrille, was in progress when Lynn presented his ticket and went in. As he stood by the wall to look on he saw Arturo Casteñada swinging a plump ranch wife of twice his age while Roger Niles was trying not to step on the feet of a slender señorita. The elite not only of Tucson but of all Arizona was there. Having been in town four days Lynn knew most of them by sight. He saw Territorial Governor John C. Frémont, famed for his conquests in California, and Chief Justice French of the Arizona Supreme Court. He knew that both of them maintained homes in Tucson although official duties kept them in Prescott most of the year. In a dance set Lynn saw the Leatherwoods and ex-Governor Safford. Leading the set was Colonel Carr of the Sixth Cavalry, Commanding Office at Fort Lowell. The fourth man in the set was his post adjutant, both officers in full dress uniform.

The quadrille ended and the next number was a waltz. As Lynn watched it a girl with flaming red hair flashed by. She was in the arms of a tall, handsome man who, by his boots and desert-cured skin, might be a ranchman. Lynn barely noticed him at first; it was the girl who held his eyes with a growing fascination. The first time she came around he thought she was beautiful. On her second circuit he knew he wanted to meet her. The third time she passed he knew he didn't want to meet, or dance with, anyone else.

The soft voice of Arturo Casteñada spoke at his elbow. 'I do not have this one, my friend. And I remember my promise. To present you to the ladies.'

'Make it just one,' Lynn said abruptly.

'That one. The girl with the blue eyes and red hair.'

Arturo followed his gaze to Judy Callahan. 'But that, I fear, will do you no good. She is the most popular of all the young *lindas* here and her card has been filled long ago. I myself tried to get a number and it was no use.'

'I want to meet her anyway,' Lynn persisted. 'How about it?'

'That, of course, can be arranged. When the music stops we will go to her.'

'Who's the tall, black-haired guy with her?'

'A neighbor to her father's ranch. His name is Larabee. Arturo lowered his voice to a tone of confidence. 'There are some who think that when she finishes this term at school she will marry him.'

The word school made Lynn remember. He'd been sitting with Roger Niles on a park bench across the street when the girl's father had delivered her to Miss Silva. Her bonnet, veil, and parasol had kept him from seeing her well that day. Now her gorgeous hair was bare and so were her arms and shoulders. Her blue eyes bright with excitement and her face turned up provocatively to her companion, to Lynn O'Hara she was the only girl on the floor.

'Are you tellin' me,' he asked with a slight frown, 'she's engaged to the guy?'

Arturo shrugged. 'Perhaps not yet. But everyone knows he's making a try for her and that he stands high with her father. The permission to let her go out with him proves it. Such permissions are rare at the Silva school.'

Lynn's frown deepened. 'Seems to me she's too young to get married.'

'In your own country to the north, perhaps yes. But down here on the border, no. The girls of our best families marry young. Do you see the couple passing us now?' Arturo indicated a middle-aged Mexican who danced by with a pretty matron of about twenty-five years. 'They are the Estavan Ochoas. When I was a boy, in the year 1871, I attended their wedding at the San Augustine Church. She was Altagracia Salazar and on the day she became Estavan's bride she was just sixteen.'

The number ended and they saw Larabee take his partner to seats by the wall. 'Come, *amigo*.' Arturo led Lynn to them.

Arturo bowed to the girl, waved a salute to Ward Larabee. 'Judy, I have the honor to present my friend Lynn O'Hara of Wyoming. He has requested it with much urgency. But I have warned him he is too late to get a number with you. Am I right?'

'Alas yes.' Judy Callahan exposed her dance schedule and Lynn saw that every line had the name of a man on it. She smiled and gave him the tips of her fingers. 'But I know much about you, Mr. O'Hara. My roommate came up from the border with you and she told me about Calabasas, and Madera, and that you're searching for a lost brother.'

'In Wyoming I work cattle for a living, Lynn said. You too live on a ranch?'

'Yes The Circle C on Cienega Creek. If you ever ride out that way, you must stop by and see my father. You'll find him as Irish as you are, Mr. O'Hara.'

'I'm riding that way tomorrow,' Lynn told her, 'on my way to the San Pedro.' He'd quite forgotten that Arturo and Larabee were with them.

Arturo recalled him to the amenities. 'And this is one of Judy's neighbors, Ward Larabee of the L Bar. Señor Larabee, my friend Lynn O'Hara.'

Larabee offered a hand. It was a firm, muscular grip and gave the impression of power in the man behind it. Yet Lynn also got the impression of a lack of warmth and sincerity. A tall, dark man with cautious eyes and a short mustache matching his close-cropped, black hair.

Immediately Lynn turned back to Judy Callahan. Since I can't dance with you, I'll stand by the wall and watch you. You don't mind?'

His admiration was so obvious that Judy colored a little. 'Why should I? I'm really flattered. Oh, hello, Archie. Yes, the next is yours.'

A cavalry captain had approached and made his presence known by offering the girl his arm. She took it and went off with him, calling back over her shoulder, 'It was nice meeting you, Mr. O'Hara. Bye.'

Arturo had to go hunting for his next partner. It left O'Hara and Larabee standing alone. 'So you're looking for a lost brother,' Larabee said. By his tone his interest was idle and impersonal. 'Read something about it in the *Citizen*, Disappeared down around Tombstone, didn't he?'

'No,' Lynn corrected, 'he'd left Tombstone and was on his way to Tucson. I'm pretty sure he was held up and robbed in the Whetstones by two men.'

'*Two* men?' Larabee waited a moment and seemed to choose his next words carefully. 'What makes you think there were *two*?'

'Because I think one of them was Ben Ubrecht and the next day Ubrecht showed up at a doctor's office with a gunshot wound in his arm. The wound had a bandage which he couldn't have wrapped and tied himself. It was made from the sleeve of a white linen shirt. Ubrecht wore a gray woolen shirt. He also got here with about half the money my brother left Tombstone with.'

Larabee changed the subject abruptly. 'Come out to the bar with me, O'Hara, and I'll buy you a drink.'

Lynn didn't want a drink. He much preferred to stay here and watch Judy dance. But she was in square set in a far corner of the room. In any case this Cienega Creek rancher might be worth talking to. He knew the country over which Lynn must travel tomorrow, on his way to the San Pedro.

So he went out with Larabee and they crossed the lobby to a crowded barroom. 'A rye highball,' Lynn said. 'The same,' Larabee echoed as he laid money on the bar.

Men lined it elbow to elbow with others at tables in the background. 'So I'm trying to run down Ubrecht,' Lynn said. 'Know him?'

'Heard of him,' Larabee said. 'But I never met him.'

'Ever run into a man they call Durango Joe?'

'I've seen him once or twice from a distance. Rides with the Clayton boys sometimes, I've heard. A good fella to stay away from. You figure he was the second of the two who held up your brother?'

'I doubt it. But he's a friend of Ubrecht's. When I braced Ubrecht the other day he got the wind up and left town. Maybe to hide for a while. Maybe at his friend Joe's shack on the San Pedro. What's the quickest way to get there?'

Larabee's eyes narrowed. His answer came with deliberation. 'The fastest way you could get there would be to follow the railroad east till you get about five miles the other side of Pantano station. Then leave the Benson road and cut southeast on a pony trail toward a high conical butte at the north tip of the Whetstones. You'll see a rock shack at the base of the butte; it's used as a sheep camp sometimes. From there the pony trail goes on southeast and strikes the

San Pedro right at Joe Dawson's homestead. Take you all day to make it, with a good horse and an early start.'

Lynn took an old envelope from his pocket and made a sketch of the route, noting the landmarks mentioned. 'Do I cross the Cienega anywhere near the Callahan ranch?'

'No. Callahan's Circle C 'd be six miles out of your way. You cross the Cienega at Pantano station on the railroad. My own place is only three miles upcreek from Pantano. Glad to have you stop in some time. Nobody there right now. I let my help come in to the *fiesta*.'

'Thanks,' Lynn said. 'So I'll ride straight to Durango Joe's. On my way back I'll take my time and stop for a call on Mr. Callahan.'

'Mike'll be glad to see you,' Larabee said aloud. His unspoken thought was: *But you won't be coming back if I can help it. You'll get no further than that sheep camp.*

Lynn failed to see the scheming in his eyes because of a surprise interruption at his other elbow. 'I made a wrong guess

153

about you, O'Hara. Owe you an apology. Had you tabbed all wrong, cowboy.'

The intruder wore a new checkered suit and a whisky flush. His eyes were bloodshot and his name was Shonsey. His outthrust hand was offering to shake O'Hara's.

Yet something in his tone made Lynn less than sure of his sincerity. 'What made you change your mind, Shonsey?'

'At Calabasas and Madera,' the man explained with something like a sheepish grin, 'I figured you for one of those thieving buckaroos who hang out at the Clayton place. I'd seen you there and I tabbed you for one of 'em. Now I know better.'

'Who told you better?' Lynn still didn't take the offered hand.

'You did, cowboy. It was part of the Clayton-Curly Max gang you shot hell out of at a water tank the other night. I mean you tipped the law on 'em and helped gun 'em down. Proves I was wrong about you. Sorry. So I made a mistake. What about another drink on me?'

'No thanks. One's enough and I've had it.' But Lynn did take the man's hand briefly. To do less would seem rude to others who were looking on.

Before sidling back to his own place at the bar Shonsey lowered his voice and gave a warning. 'Watch out for the Curly Max boys, fella. They'll be layin' for you from now on, account of you gettin' their pals shot up.'

'They're a long way off,' Lynn said with a shrug. It was eighty miles to Charleston and more than a hundred to Galeyville.

'Not all of 'em.' Shonsey dropped a sly lid over one of his bloodshot eyes. 'A few of 'em came up here to take in the *fiesta*. Bad *hombres* who'll be sore as hell about what happened to Dick Gray and Chuck Snow and Frankie Byers. I'd stay away from the *fiesta* grounds the next coupla days if I was you.'

'Thanks for the tip, Shonsey. Happens I'll be out of town the next two-three days.' Lynn finished his drink and turned to Larabee. 'What do you say we go back to the frolic?'

'Have to, myself,' Larabee said. 'Got the next number with the colonel's wife.' They recrossed the lobby to the ball-room Just as a new dance was starting.

Lynn saw the yellow-haired head of Roger Niles weaving through the crowd and in a moment Niles joined him. 'No rest for the weary,' the reporter said wryly. 'A knifing a night in the *Barrio*, they say, and it turns out tonight's no exception. My cruel editor just sent word that I have to go cover it.'

'Too bad,' Lynn murmured.

'Too bad for me and too good for you,' Roger corrected. 'Means I have to cut dance number eight with Judy Callahan. Heard she turned you down on account of a full card. Now you can grab number eight if you talk fast. Have to scoot along now.'

The reporter scurried off to cover a *Barrio* knifing. And Lynn, hardly believing his luck, stood watching Judy Callahan as she paced through a qua-drille with a man old enough to be her grandfather. He happened to be one of her own father's close friends, Peter Kitchen of the Potrero Ranch near the border.

When the set ended Lynn raced to her. Her hand was still on Kitchen's arm as she looked up in surprise at Lynn's eager face. 'You had the next one with Roger Niles?'

As she nodded he told her that Roger had been sent suddenly on an assignment. 'So I was hoping . . .'

'Of course you may have it, Lynn O'Hara. Thank you, Uncle Pete. You must come to us on the Cienega and pay us a long visit.' She transferred her hand from the older man's arm to Lynn's.

He was walking her toward a punch bowl when the music started again. Immediately she stopped and clapped her hands. 'We mustn't miss this. It is what we call the cradle dance. You know it?'

'You'll have to show me,' Lynn admitted. 'Reckon it never got as far north as Wyoming.'

'We loop our hands behind each other, like this.' Judy linked her fingers behind Lynn, stood toe to toe with him as she leaned far back. When he took the same relative position their bodies made a deep V, or cradle. 'Now we dance in circles,' she directed. 'It's not difficult. The feet just follow the music.'

To Lynn's surprise he managed fairly well. Watching the other couples he saw that it was a whirling dance, the whirls always in the same direction. The swift movement of it billowed Judy's full ruffled skirt and made it boil about her ankle. He could feel the full warm weight of her against the loop of his hands. 'You learn quickly, Lynn O'Hara.'

The music's tempo quickened. By the time they'd circled the floor twice Judy's cheeks were a radiant crimson and Lynn himself was out of breath. And still they whirled, around and around in a stream of fifty other couples doing the same, feet close together and heads at arm's length apart.

'I'd do better in a square set,' Lynn

said.

She laughed at him across the wide top of their arms, her loveliness in just the right focus from his eyes. Again they circled the floor and beyond her, standing against a wall, Lynn glimpsed her escort Ward Larabee. Larabee was watching them intently and it struck Lynn that the man's gaze was unfriendly.

He recalled what Arturo had said and suddenly Lynn himself felt an unreasonable unfriendliness toward Larabee. He'd known this girl for less than an hour and yet he knew he wanted her for himself. She was the one he'd been waiting for all his life. Was it true that Larabee had been hand-picked by her father? In any case Lynn knew that he himself must lose no time making friends with rancher Mike Callahan.

The orchestra stopped and Lynn, along with men, applauded lustily for an encore.

When it came the tempo was waltz time and here Lynn was not without experience. This way he could hold her a little closer and feel her hand upon his shoulder. And this time the pace was slow enough to allow breath for talking. 'Sometimes,' he suggested cautiously, 'you spend a week end with your father at the ranch?'

'But of course,' she said. 'He has no one but me and he is lonely out there. So every third Friday afternoon he drives in to get me and I have two days and nights with him. He brings me back to the school late Sunday.'

'So I'll drop in to see him myself,' Lynn decided craftily.

'You will? When?'

Lynn looked at her with a straight face. 'Why not three Saturdays from now?'

They circled the floor before she spoke again. 'You're a friend of Roger Niles, are you not?'

'Sure. Roger and I get along fine.'

'I think he likes my roommate, Gracie Casteñada,' Judy confided. 'Miss Silva has very strict rules; so he cannot see her at the school.'

'Doesn't seem hardly fair,' Lynn

murmured.

'So the next week end I spend at the ranch,' Judy said 'perhaps I'll take Gracie with me. She's a ranch girl of Mexico and she'll feel at home on the Circle C. We've a pretty little pony for her to ride there.'

A hint of conspiracy in Judy's tone belied the studied innocence in her blue eyes and Lynn could hardly miss it. He was about to follow up eagerly when she changed the subject. 'Have you learned anything more about what happened to your brother?'

'I think so,' Lynn told her. 'And I'm heading for the San Pedro tomorrow to find out more.' He must pretend not to know she'd opened a door for him. And for Roger Niles. It must seem to be a mere happenstance when he and Roger stopped by the Circle C on a week end when Judy was entertaining a schoolmate there. If Miss Silva should ever find out about it, how could she say that it had been planned in advance?

In all it gave Lynn a glow inside and

he drew Judy a little closer until he could feel her soft hair brush his cheek. His had been a grim and lonely mission this last month, riding from town to town searching for a lost brother. It was a mission he could forget, for the moment, with this lovely girl in his arms. Beyond her at the wall again he saw Ward Larabee with an unsmiling gaze fixed upon them.

* * *

At the same moment, in a cantina of the *Barrio Libre*, Ace Shonsey leaned across a table in furtive talk with two men who would have been unwelcome at any of the better Congress Street bars. The heavily stupid and unshaven face of one made him look like a common tramp; the other, slim and dark and sly, could be a back alley footpad. They were protesting that a price just offered was not enough.

'But it's plenty,' Shonsey insisted. 'I'm not asking you to slit his throat. Just beat him up on his way home tonight. Spoil his looks a little.'

'Like he did yours?' the sly man smirked staring at a bruise around Shonsey's mouth.

The gambler repeated his offer. 'A hundred dollars. Fifty apiece for you. I guarantee he's not wearing a gun tonight. The two of you can jump him on his way to the Palace.'

'He'll figger it was you,' the heavy man said, 'who sicked us onto him.'

Shonsey drooped a wise eyelid. 'No he won't. I pretended to go soft on him and he fell for it. Everybody'll figure it was a couple of the Curly Max gang getting even with him for what happened at the water tank. Besides the hundred bucks, you can pick up whatever he's got in his wallet. Lay for him in the doorway of that empty warehouse just above Zechendorf's on Main. He has to pass it on his way from the Cosmopolitan to the Palace.'

A beer later the slim man agreed. 'It's a deal, Shonsey.'

# 11

The time was nearing midnight as Altagracia Casteñada stood at a dark window in the upper room she shared with Judy Callahan, watching the street, fearfully hoping she'd been wrong and that a second look at Judy's escort would reassure her. According to the rules of the school she should have been asleep for two hours. But she'd been much too harassed to sleep. It seemed fantastically impossible that Judy could be out with a thief and a killer. Now she must make sure. She must see the man's face again when, at midnight, he brought Judy home from the ball.

All the other girls at the school had been in bed since ten. Only Altagracia stood in her night robe watching the street. The man was sure to come on time because he'd hardly risk the displeasure of Miss Silva. He'd be wanting to take Judy out again some time.

At a minute before twelve Altagracia heard the clop-clop of horses trot up Convent Street. The door lamp below was still lighted and she could see the carriage as it drew up at the block. The tall, caped escort got out and helped Judy to the walk. By the lilt of her laugh Altagracia could tell that she'd had a grand time. But the man wore his wide-brimmed hat and it kept her, at the oblique angle of her vision, from seeing his upper face.

They came through the picket gate and up a brick walk to the door. At once it opened and Altagracia heard the voice of Miss Silva. The headmistress was taking no chances and had waited up for them. The man spoke heartily, 'Here we are, Miss Silva, right on time like I promised.'

'It was a wonderful party!' This happily from Judy Callahan.

An exchange of goodnights was cut short by Miss Silva just as a bell on the Church Plaza struck twelve. Altagracia heard the door close and saw the escort walk back to his carriage. She herself scurried to bed so that Judy wouldn't catch her spying. She didn't dare accuse the man — yet. There was still a chance that she'd been mistaken. She couldn't confide her suspicions either to Judy or to Miss Silva until she was absolutely sure.

Yet someone, the girl thought wretchedly, *must* be told. It must be someone close to her whose confidence she could trust. Her father Don Vincente had gone back to Magdalena. What about her cousin Arturo? Arturo was an officer of the law. He was a young man of the world who knew the ways of men like Ward Larabee. She decided to confide in Arturo and in no one else — at least until she could get another look at Ward Larabee's face.

★ ★ ★

At the Palace Hotel Larabee dismissed his carriage and went up to his room. Minutes later he came back down to the lobby with a packed bag and checked

166

out. 'Got to be at the L Bar bright and early,' he explained to the night clerk. 'So I'm hitting the trail right now.'

He walked rapidly to the Lexington livery stable and ordered the night hostler to saddle his horse. By one o'clock he was on his way, taking the Benson road which followed the Southern Pacific rails easterly out of town. He hadn't planned this. He'd hoped to sleep late and ride leisurely home by sunlight.

A new consideration had changed his mind. It demanded his immediate attention and until it was taken care of he could have no peace. He wasn't much afraid of the sheriff's crew. They had too many other manhunts occupying them to give much thought to a mysterious disappearance three months old. But that young cowboy from Wyoming was something else. He was nose down to the trail of Ubrecht and not likely to be shaken off until he ran the man down. Early tomorrow morning he'd be riding to Durango Joe's and he might well find Ubrecht hiding there. Ubrecht with nearly half of the Milton O'Hara loot still on him! Larabee reasoned fearfully that exposure of Ubrecht might lead to the exposure of himself.

Two things could be done to make things safe and Ward Larabee, as he spurred impatiently along the Benson road, knew that he could do them only by keeping well ahead of O'Hara.

Fourteen miles out of Tucson he came to the rail station of Papago, near the Vail ranch. Labaree cantered by it in the dark without stopping. Four miles beyond it he came to the depot of Pantano where the track crossed Cienega Creek on a trestle.

It was now past four o'clock and pink was tinting the eastern sky.

Here Larabee left the Benson road and spurred his mount three miles up creek to the L Bar. Again he found it deserted, his Mexican help still being away at the Tucson *fiesta*. Larabee grained his horse and made himself breakfast. While the coffee boiled he went to a duffel bag and fished from it a white linen shirt with a left sleeve cut from it. Until Lynn O'Hara had mentioned a bandage, it hadn't occurred to Larabee that a strip of linen bound around Joe Dawsons bloody arm could be identified as part of a shirt sleeve.

Now he burned it in the kitchen stove.

The important thing was still to be done. The sun was an hour high when Larabee resaddled his horse. There was no great hurry, because Lynn O'Hara right now would be just starting out from town. He wouldn't get as far as the sheep camp before early afternoon.

Ward Larabee slipped his late model 44-40 centerfire Winchester rifle into the saddle scabbard. Most of the riders on this range were still using the old .44 rimfire models and this one was far more accurate. Larabee mounted and rode east from the L Bar until he struck a pony trail which ran southeast toward a conical butte at the northerly tip of the Whetstones.

This was the trail along which Lynn O'Hara would ride later today, on his way to the San Pedro cabin of Durango Joe Dawson.

The more he thought about it, the more Larabee was sure that getting rid of O'Hara was a must. He himself would never be linked with it. People would think it was a reprisal from the Curly Max clique of outlaws. A clannish lot, those follows and as ruthless as sharks. They'd never forget that five of their number had been shot down at the Rillito tank in a coup for which the Wyoming cowboy more than anyone else had been responsible. It would only take one of them to do it. And one bullet. Any one of forty horse thieves from Galeyville or Charleston could have been taking in the Tucson *fiesta* along with Charley Snow and the others. He could easily have learned that O'Hara was riding today to look for Ubrecht at Durango Joe's. The cowboy had made no secret of it. So if he should be dry-gulched on the way, why would anyone suspect Ward Larabee?

The L Bar man took his time and it was late morning when he arrived at the rock shack sometimes used by a sheepherder. He should be at least two or three hours ahead of O'Hara. A deep desert arroyo ran back of the shack and Larabee concealed his mount in it. With his rifle he walked back to the shack and took a position of ambush there. The place had a small paneless window which faced the pony trail and was less than sixty yards from it.

Larabee cleaned the bore of his centerfire weapon and made sure the magazine was full of shells. He pumped one of them into the chamber and waited patiently for O'Hara. At sixty yards how could he miss?

★   ★   ★

The afternoon passed and O'Hara didn't come by. As the day faded Larabee waited with a growing nervousness. When the sun dipped back of the Empire Hills he still waited. O'Hara, tired from being up late at a dance, could have stayed in bed all morning and be until nightfall getting this far.

But when darkness came Lynn O'Hara's white-stockinged roan still hadn't come along the pony trail. And if it came now the darkness would cheat a sniper's aim. When nothing was left but starlight Larabee gave up and went to the arroyo for his horse. He concluded that O'Hara had decided to rest a day in town and make the San Pedro ride tomorrow.

It was nearly midnight when Larabee got back to the L Bar. In a sullen mood he fed himself and his horse. In the morning he must go back to the sheep camp and try again.

At sunrise he was up and getting his breakfast. An hour later he again saddled up for a ride to the sheep camp ambush. Then he saw a horseman coming upcreek from the direction of Pantano.

The man drew up and proved to be Jock Anson who rode for Mike Callahan's Circle C. Anson stopped to twist a cigaret and pass the time of day. 'Hi, neighbor; saw you at the fandango in town the other evenin', didn't I?'

Larabee nodded. 'Yeh, had to come

home and look after my stock. Help's at the *fiesta*.'

'Got to get home myself,' Anson said. 'Mike's all alone and he needs me.'

'Anything new happen in town,' Larabee asked, 'since I left?'

'Not much. The usual devilment they always have at *fiesta* time. A few footpad jobs and a knifing in the *Barrio*. Couple of thugs jumped that cowboy from Wyoming and beat the tar out of him, night before last. He was on his way home from the *baile*.'

So that explained why O'Hara hadn't ridden to the San Pedro yesterday!

'Beat him up?' Larabee prompted. 'Who do they think did it?'

'They figger it was a coupla border outlaws gettin' even with him for what happened at the Rillito tank. Marked him up good, they did, and put him out of circulation for a coupla days. Jumped him as he was passin' a warehouse doorway just above Zechendorf's on Main. You'd think they'd've pistol-whipped him or knifed him. But all they did was beat hell out of him and leave him lay there. Well, so long, neighbor; got to push on to the ranch.'

It changed Larabee's plans. No use lying in wait any more at the sheep camp. If he got O'Hara at all it would have to be in town. He wondered why the two thugs had let O'Hara off with a mere beating. Was it a get-even job by border outlaws? If it was a footpad job they would take O'Hara's wallet. Had they? If the cowboy was stripped of his cash he'd need to get paying work somewhere. And that would slow him up in his chase after Ubrecht.

Impatience to find out exactly the condition of Lynn O'Hara and his immediate plans sent Larabee riding, not toward the sheep camp, but back toward Tucson. This distance was twenty-one miles and he made it by early afternoon. Again he registered at the Palace.

'Hear one of our guests got beat up the other night!' he remarked to the lobby clerk.

'You heard right, Mr. Larabee. He's in

room 26 and they say he'll be laid up for another day or two. Those buggers worked him over right good.'

'Snatched his wallet, I suppose?'

The clerk grinned and shook his head. 'Nope. City Marshal Brokow posted a warning about footpads. Advised *fiesta* guests to leave their pokes in the hotel safes when they went out at night. This cowboy had the good sense to do that when he went out to the *baile*. So all he lost was some skin and blood.'

Larabee went up to his own room and from there stepped a few doors down the hall to look in on Lynn O'Hara. The Wyoming man was propped up in his bed, dressed except for his shirt and boots, a pillow stuffed behind his back while he read the current *Citizen*. His forehead was bandaged, his chin had a strip of court plaster, and his swollen left cheek showed a blue-black bruise.

'Looks like you've been fighting a buzz-saw.' Larabee used a tone of light banter. 'How you doing?'

'I can still take nourishment,' Lynn

told him with a grin. 'Be on my feet in a day or two. I'd be up right now except for Doc Handy. He makes me out worse'n I am. Thought you'd left town, Larabee.'

'Only for a day. Had a chore or two at the ranch. Just heard about those border boys working you over. Did you get a look at 'em?'

'They came at me from behind,' Lynn said. 'Beaned me before I could turn around. Hi there, Arturo. Come on in.' Deputy Arturo Casteñada had appeared in the doorway.

'I cannot stay but a minute, *amigo*. Just want to see how you are mending.' The young Mexican waved a hand toward Ward Larabee. 'My salutes to you also, señor.'

And mine to you,' Larabee murmured.

'Nice of both of you to drop in,' Lynn said. 'Take a chair, Arturo, and tell us the news of the town.'

But Arturo remained standing. 'I cannot delay, señores. Am on my way to see my cousin at the Silva school. She has sent for me to come at once.'

Lynn regarded him curiously. 'Didn't know they let men-folks in that place.'

'I, who am her blood cousin, am an exception,' Arturo explained. 'The matter is of extreme importance, she says, and they will permit me to visit her briefly in the parlor.' His face wore a puzzled look. 'It is a strange matter which I do not understand.'

'Yeh?' Lynn prompted. 'What's strange about it?'

Arturo took from his pocket a note which he had just received from Altagracia by special messenger. It was in Spanish and he translated it aloud:

*Muy primo mio*:
   Please consult with me at once on a matter of importance. It concerns something which I have seen from my window. Very much I need your confidence and advice.
                    *Prima suya*,
                              Altagracia.

177

Lynn looked from Arturo to Larabee and back to Arturo. Both men seemed disturbed and to a degree shocked. 'Something she saw from her window!' Lynn puzzled. 'Which window? The one at Calabasas where she saw the horse thief who shot Morales?'

'I cannot believe it was that one,' Arturo murmured. 'Perhaps she means the one at the school.'

A quick, strained protest came from Ward Larabee. 'What could she see from there — except the street in front?'

With a Latin shrug and a spread of his palms Arturo gave it up. 'That is what mystifies me, señores. Surely she would see no evil on Convent Street, where live only gentle people. I go now to consult with her, as she requests. *Hasta la vista, amigos.*'

# 12

Michael Callahan, a short-stemmed pipe between his teeth, sat comfortably under a sun-shade on the roof of the Circle C ranch house. It was a flat roof with a parapet wall on all sides. The parapet had loopholes for rifles and more than a few times Callahan and his crew had used them to stand off raiding Apaches. For the same defensive purpose the house itself had outer walls which were three adobe bricks thick. Many an arrow head and bullet was embedded in them.

Right now on this Tuesday evening, September seventh, the scene was peaceful. Callahan, a stocky, solid cattleman with a rusty stubble of beard, looked out across a plain of cacti and brown grass toward the Empire Hills which fenced his range on the west. Cienega Creek ran only a hundred yards in front of his house, with just a trickle of flow this late in the season. But above the corrals

Callahan had dammed the stream to make a five-acre pond, always insuring stock water, and around this pond young cottonwoods made an oval of green.

Time was when Mike Callahan had kept a lookout posted on this roof day and night, alert for marauders. Sometimes the marauders had been renegade Apaches truant from a reservation. Of late they'd been more often men of his own race stock thieves from the so-called 'cowboy' ranches of the upper San Pedro. Twice this season he'd lost a few horses to them; and once a dozen of his fat steers had been run off by night, perhaps to be butchered and sold in the meat shops of Charleston.

Right now Callahan's own crew was out rounding up a bunch of fall beef which had been contracted for by the government and which next month must be delivered on the hoof to feed Indians at the San Carlos Reservation. Looking westward from the roof Callahan could see the brown hills where his crew was now camped.

Also he saw three horsemen approaching from the west. The tallest of them, on a blaze-faced roan with white stockings, rode like a cattle hand. Each of the trio wore gun-belt and had a carbine in his saddle scabbard. Since it was possible that they were hostile, Mike Callahan alertly picked up his own repeating rifle which was never far from his hand.

Then, as he recognized one of the three oncomers, he relaxed. That young Spanish deputy of Sheriff Shibell's, Arturo Casteñada, was his very good friend. Callahan got up and moved to a roof well which gave to steep steps. These he descended to the hard-packed earthen floor of his house.

A few minutes later he was in his barnyard greeting three arrivals. '*Bien venida*, Arturo. I am lonesome and will welcome guests. You will stay the night?'

'You do not have to ask us twice, Don Miguel. May I present my friends Wally Whorton and Lynn O'Hara? Señor Whorton is a special agent of the Southern Pacific and his mission is to catch two men and recover a payroll they stole at Benson. Señor O'Hara is from Wyoming and he is . . . '

'I know what you're here for, O'Hara my lad,' Callahan broke in heartily. 'Read about it in the papers. You want to find out what happened to your brother back in May. Anything I can do to help, just say the word. Glad to see all of you.' The ranchman clapped his hands and it brought his Indian cook to the house door. 'Supper and beds for three guests, Huachuco,' he shouted.

When the horses were stalled and fed Callahan led his visitors to the house. Huachuco brought *refrescos* and while they waited for supper the four men sat in a cool, adobe room with Indian rugs on the clay floor and whose thick adobe walls, like the roof parapets, had loopholes for defense.

'My daughter Judy,' Callahan said to Lynn O'Hara, 'spoke of you in a letter which came today. Said she met you at a party only a few hours before a couple of bruisers jumped you on a dark street.'

Lynn admitted it ruefully. His head bandage was gone but a plaster strip still crossed his chin, reaching obliquely to a bruise on his cheek.

'Sheriff Shibell sends us on a special mission,' Arturo explained. 'Mr. Whorton has arrived from San Francisco hoping to detect and prosecute the Benson robbers and recover thirty-two thousand dollars for the railroad. The sheriff assigns me to help and guide him. We have warrants to search the cabins of several logical suspects and the first of these is Joe Dawson who lives on the San Pedro below Contention City.'

Lynn added a word of his own. 'I'm trying to run down a man named Ubrecht, who might be hiding at Dawson's. So the sheriff told me to go along with Arturo and Whorton.'

'A wise precaution,' Callahan remarked bluntly. 'It might need three of you to walk in at a place like Dawson's. They call him Durango Joe and sometimes he hangs out with Old Man Clayton's cow thieves further up the river.' The Circle C man looked shrewdly at a deputy badge on Lynn's jacket. 'You figure maybe Ben Ubrecht knows what happened to your brother?'

'I'd bet on it,' Lynn said, and explained why.

Huachuco appeared and announced supper. They went into another cool, adobe room and sat down to boiled mutton, cornbread, and chokecherry wine.

'About the Benson robbery,' Callahan said to the railroad's special agent. 'You got anything to go on?'

Wally Whorton nodded. 'We happen to know that the stolen money included two packages of new ten dollar bills, fifty bills to a package and numbered consecutively. Means a hundred of the bills can be identified.'

'So if you find one of 'em on Durango Joe, he's your man.'

'He's one of our men. There were two. If we fail to find anything at the Dawson place, we'll search at other ranches up the river.'

'Also,' Arturo put in, 'we will go to

Tombstone and see if any of the new tens has been spent there. The Earp brothers are friendly to us and perhaps will help. They do not like the Curly Max and Clem Clayton people. Sheriff Shibell suggests that we look at money spent at the Bird Cag Theater and at the main gambling saloons. Later we must do the same at Charleston.'

'It'll take more than the three of you,' Callahan warned dourly, 'to shake down Charleston.'

Arturo gave one of his Latin shrugs. 'Three of us are all that Shibell can spare. Much other evil is abroad that he needs to expose and punish. He still has not caught the thieves who murdered Pancho Morales at Calabasas.'

Soon after supper the two older men, Callahan and Whorton, retired. The younger ones, O'Hara and Casteñada, went up on the roof to enjoy the coolness of night.

'You kinda gave me the brush-off, Arturo,' Lynn said as he rolled a cigaret, 'when I asked what your little cousin wanted to tell you at the school. Something she saw from her window, her note said.'

Again Arturo tried to disparage it. 'My cousin is very young,' he said, 'and she has little experience with men. From her window at Calabasas she saw the face of a killer. From her window at the Silva school she saw another face and imagined it was the same one. But I am certain she is mistaken. The man she names is a *caballero* of honor and high repute, a friend of mine and of the best people in Arizona. To class him as a common corral thief is not to be thought of. I have scolded my cousin and made her promise not to speak of it to others. Nor have I myself reported her message to the sheriff.'

Lynn blew a thoughtful smoke ring. 'Suppose she's right and you're wrong, Arturo.'

'But that is impossible! The man she names is one of position and high character, esteemed by the best families like the Saffords and the Ochoas. He does

186

not fit such a cheap crime as stealing horses from a corral. The thief's hat was shot with a bullet hole, remember, so he had to throw it away. Our posse picks it up and sees that it was purchased at Tombstone where many cowboy outlaws do their trading. The man named by my foolish little cousin lives far from Tombstone and does his trading in Tucson.'

'You mean you haven't even asked him for an alibi?'

'That much I did,' Arturo said. 'The raid at Calabasas was a minute before midnight Sunday. I asked him in confidence where he was Monday morning. He told me that he was at his ranch which is more than a day's ride from Calabasas.'

'Was anyone with him at his ranch Monday morning?'

'His help was in town at the *fiesta*. But a caller came by that day and took lunch with him. A well known and popular prospector named Packsaddle Jones. He is very religious and a friend of the priests at San Xavier Mission. What he says is certain to be the truth.'

'You checked the man's alibi with this Packsaddle Jones?'

'Not yet. But I will. When he nooned at my friend's ranch a week ago he was on his way to prospect in the Dragoons, not far from Tombstone. As a matter of routine I shall look him up at the first opportunity and have him confirm the alibi. Let us not speak of it any more, Lynn O'Hara.'

Lynn didn't speak of it any more but after going to bed he thought about it. How sound would the alibi be even if Packsaddle Jones sincerely confirmed it? A week had already passed and more days would pass before the prospector could be found and questioned. To a wandering rock hunter one day would be the same as another. He'd remember stopping at a ranch and be grateful for a noon meal given him there. When asked if it happened on a certain Monday as the host claimed, he'd hardly deny the date. Perhaps he'd really stopped there on a Wednesday or a Tuesday. But if the kind rancher said it was Monday, he'd probably agree without a quibble.

Lynn lay abed, pondering it. Had Altagracia been mistaken — or had she actually seen the same face twice?

★ ★ ★

After an early breakfast Callahan's three overnight guests rode on toward the San Pedro. Lynn O'Hara, as straight as a cavalryman in the saddle, rode between Arturo and the small, wiry man who wore the badge of a railroad's special agent. Wally Whorton wasn't toughened to long riding and the strain of it showed on him by the time they reached an abandoned sheep camp at the north tip of the Whetstones.

'How much further?' he asked Arturo.

'Two hours yet,' he was told. 'You wish to rest here?'

The railroad man wanted very much to rest but was too proud to admit it. They pushed on southeast toward Joe Dawson's place. 'Is there reason to believe,'

Lynn asked, 'that he was in on the Benson job?'

'Only that it would have been convenient for him,' Arturo said. 'His place is not far upriver from Benson and the robbers escaped in that direction. Also he has often consorted with cattle thieves and stage robbers.'

'If Dawson was one of the Benson robbers,' Lynn reminded him, 'the man who sided him wasn't Ubrecht. It happened just before midnight Tuesday and we know Ubrecht was playing cards at the Tucson *fiesta* all that night.'

They rode on across a flat of ocotillo and greasewood. At the east edge of it Lynn saw a line of cottonwoods which marked the San Pedro. Beyond the river loomed a range of mountains which had to be the Dragoons, long a stronghold of Apache war parties. It was there, Lynn knew, that rich silver strikes had been made recently as a result of which smelters were now operating at both Contention and Tombstone.

'When they get the silver smelted,'

Lynn asked as they jogged along, 'where do they take it?'

'They take it by Wells Fargo state to Benson,' Wally Whorton told him, 'then by the Southern Pacific to San Francisco, then east by the Union Pacific and on to Philadelphia. This year more than a million in silver bullion will go that way from the smelters of the Tombstone district.'

'Doesn't that stage ever get held up, on its run to Benson?'

'Sometimes. But silver bars don't make very good stage robber bait. They're too heavy to ride fast with. Road agents'd rather have cash — like the payroll the two guys grabbed at Benson.'

They rode on and struck the river a little below the Joe Dawson homestead. This late in the year the stream was shallow and they splashed across to the east bank. After rounding an upriver bend they sighted a corral and two unpainted frame buildings — a cabin and a shed.

The cabin's pipe chimney had a curl of smoke. 'So he is home,' Arturo said. 'Let us hope he has company by the name of Ubrecht.'

In case Durango Joe had more than one outlaw guest the three lawmen drew rifles from their saddle scabbards and closed in on the cabin from as many directions. Lynn stopped his horse about ten yards in front of the door. 'You at home, Dawson?' he yelled. 'Come on out.'

The man who stepped out was short, thick-set, shaggy, baggily dressed and had broad, rounded shoulders. He was unarmed and seemed surprised rather than alarmed. 'Yeh? What do yuh want?' His eyes shifted from badge to badge of his callers.

'Is Obrecht in there?' Lynn asked him.

'You mean Ben Ubrecht? Nope. Ain't seen him in a month of Sundays. What do yuh want with him?'

'I want to ask him where he hid my brother's body.'

'You mean you're that cowboy from Wyoming? Read about you. Come in and take a look, if you want.'

Whorton and Casteñada dismounted and advanced to the door. There Arturo displayed a search warrant. And Whorton challenged, 'You wouldn't happen to have any of the Benson payroll money stashed here, would you?'

The fact that Durango Joe didn't look a bit worried convinced Lynn that nothing would be found in the cabin. He himself remained on alert watch outside while Arturo and Whorton went in to make a search. If Durango Joe had a split of the Benson money he'd probably buried it at a distance from his cabin.

Lynn looked about him to see where such a hiding place might be. The corral had two loose horses. Both of them could be Dawson's; or one of them might be Ubrecht's. Up and down the river any one of several cottonwood groves might hide either Ubrecht or the stolen money.

Nearer, to the left of the shed, Lynn saw a mound of clay with an oblique door on it. He supposed it was a potato cellar. Most isolated ranches had a root cellar, sometimes used as a shelter in storms.

On an impulse Lynn rode his horse to this one and dismounted. The ground about it was hard gravel and showed no tracks. The slanting door had a hasp and padlock but wasn't locked. It could only be locked from the outside. If a man went down there to hide he'd be unable to lock the door behind him.

Was Ubrecht staying here with Dawson? Had he seen three strangers coming upriver and to avoid them had he slipped down into a root cellar?

Lynn drew his holster gun and went to the door. He took a grip on the hasp and raised the door open. All he could see was a narrow well and deep wooden steps descending into darkness.

'Anybody home?' he called.

No answer. But it proved nothing. A man hiding down there would lie doggo in the dark.

There was only one way to find out. Lynn cocked his gun and stepped into the entrance well. After one step down he used his left hand to strike a match.

He tossed the flaming match into the cellar; but as it hit the damp floor it went out. Its brief flare had revealed nothing.

Again Lynn took a cautious step downward. This time it brought a roar and a flash of gunfire from below. A bullet burned Lynn's cheek. He began tripping his trigger, once, twice, three times, shooting obliquely down at where the gun had flashed.

After three shots he took another step down and then fired twice more.

A thin groan meant that the man was hit. Lynn reloaded his gun and moved on down to the cellar floor.

The flare of his match showed him Ubrecht. The man sprawled helpless with blood on his head and breast. Lynn struck another match, saw the stub of a candle, and lighted it.

A quick examination told him that Ubrecht had been hit twice fatally and would soon stop breathing. There could only be a minute or two to question him. Lynn kneeled by him and asked urgently:

'You've got nothing more to lose now, Ubrecht; who helped you hold up my brother?'

The man's lips moved but made no sound. Lynn tried again. 'Who cut the sleeve out of his shirt to bind up your arm?'

When there was still no answer Lynn took a wallet from the man's hip pocket and counted the money in it. The total came to about nineteen hundred dollars. His split of the take from Milton O'Hara would have been twenty-two hundred and since then he could have spent about a hundred a month at Tucson.

'What did you do with his body, Ubrecht?'

Again the lips moved and this time Lynn caught a word or two. He couldn't be sure whether they were meant to reveal or to deceive. 'A mine shaft . . . the *Vulcan* . . . '

It was all Ubrecht had the strength for. His eyes took a deathly stare and when Lynn felt of his heart there was no beat. Arturo Casteñada, drawn by the sound of shots, called from above, 'What goes down there?'

'Ubrecht,' Lynn called back.

# 13

The San Pedro, flowing north from the border, offered the best bottomland in all of southeastern Arizona. The railroad crossed it at Benson and above Benson a dozen small ranches spotted the valley, some of them shoestring layouts like Durango Joe Dawson's. 'Ten miles above Dawson's place a rider in the year 1880 would come to the smelter town of Contention, where the stage road left the river and turned east toward the region's fast growing boom city of Tombstone, at the southerly tip of the Dragoons.

If a rider continued another ten miles upriver from Contention he would come to a brand new silver smelter with a wooden bridge joining it to the town of Charleston. And still another hour's ride upriver would take him to Old Man Clayton's ranch, notorious as a rendezvous for border thieves. Many raids had been laid to Clem Clayton and his three gunslung sons, and to the half-gambler, half-cowboy crew who rode for them. Often they'd been hauled into court but always there were perjured alibis; never had there been an important conviction.

A day after the shooting of Ben Ubrecht in Joe Dawson's root cellar, six men were sharing a pitcher of beer in a cottonwood grove back of Old Man Clayton's ranch house. The heavy-set man with curly brown hair spoke in a tone of righteous complaint. 'They blame everything on us, Clem, whether we do it or not.'

Old Man Clayton bobbed his white-haired head and agreed peevishly. He was the only man in the group over fifty. 'You said it, Max. Accordin' to Lucky here, they're layin' the Benson payroll job on us and we don't even know who done it.'

Lucky Luke Bundy, a pock-marked gambler, had just returned from Tucson with the latest gossip. 'Not only that, but they're layin' the Calabasas job onto you too, Clem. Either on you or on Curly's boys.' Bundy thumbed toward the heavy-set man whose name was Max Broccardi and who was known far and wide as Curly Max.

Curly spat angrily. 'And my boys weren't within sixty mile of either job.'

Ike Clayton, eldest of Clem's three sons, snapped his suspenders and tilted his chair back. 'What burns me up, Pop, is us lettin' that Wyoming cowboy O'Hara spy on us while he was pretendin' to put up hay. Turns out he did some more spyin' at Tucson. Spotted Pardee and Snow and the others in a beer garden riggin' up Gil Stilwell's rescue at the depot; and he spoiled it.'

'He sure did,' Bundy confirmed. 'He tipped the sheriff's office and they switched plans. Later he helped burn down our boys at a water tank.'

'Some day we'll get him for it,' Clem Clayton swore savagely. 'Pass the word on it, Walt,' he added to his tallest son. 'I want that cowboy gunned out of his saddle on sight. The damned snooper! Ten to one it's him who's tryin' to lay the Benson job onto us.'

Bundy didn't think so. 'The only job he's interested in is findin' out what happened to his brother Milt back in May. The word is he suspects Ben Ubrecht and is hot on his tail right now.'

Roy Clayton, Clem's youngest son, had a smooth face and tawny hair parted in the middle. He liked loud shirts and sometimes worked as a bartender at the Last Chance saloon on the Tombstone-Charleston road. 'Ben Ubrecht usta ride with us,' he reminded them. 'So did his side kick Joe Dawson. Lately they've made a tie-up with somebody else. Wouldn't be surprised if it was the same somebody who did all three of those jobs they're tryin' to lay onto us. Calabasas, Benson, and knockin' over Milt O'Hara back in May.'

'And us clean on all three of 'em!' Curly Max Broccardi made the protest piously although he was entirely without conscience, with no more respect for human life than for a fly crawling across his plate. All six of these men had taken part in the infamous massacre at Fronteras, across the border, shooting from ambush into sixteen peaceful Mexican traders.

'Who's that comin'?' Ike Clayton looked alertly toward a rider who approached from downriver.

'Looks like Johnnie-behind-the-Deuce,' his brother Walt said.

Johnnie O'Rourke, with a nickname acquired, from his habit of always backing a Two-spot whenever it showed in a faro layout, rode up and dismounted with a smirk. Usually he could be found playing cards at the Last Chance but sometimes he came here to curry favor with the Claytons.

'Heard the latest?' he asked them.

'If you know anything,' Clem demanded, 'spill it.'

'Three lawmen from the county seat,' O'Rourke told them, 'just raided Joe Dawson's place down the river. They found Ben Ubrecht there with half of the Milt O'Hara money on him. One of the lawmen was O'Hara's brother from

Wyoming and he gunned Ubrecht dead.'

Clem Clayton chewed on it for a moment. 'Who were the other two lawmen?'

'A special agent of the Southern Pacific and a county deputy named Casteñada. They were lookin' for the Benson payroll money in case Dawson was in on that trick. Didn't find any of it.'

'Where are they now?' Broccardi asked sharply. 'I mean the three lawmen.'

'They pinched Dawson on a charge of harborin' a criminal. Casteñada took him to Benson along with Ubrecht's body. He'll take Dawson on to Tucson by train. The Southern Pacific man'll stay at the Dawson place for a couple of days diggin' around for the payroll loot. It was a two-man job; so if Joe was in on it there oughta be sixteen thousand dollars stashed on his land there.'

'What about the Wyoming cowboy? You say he's wearin' a badge now?'

The newsmonger nodded. 'O'Hara picked up an Indian guide and a pack mule and started for the *Vulcan* mine in the Whetstones. Somethin' Ubrecht said just before he cashed his chips made O'Hara think his brother's body was dropped down that shaft. It's a deserted mine and only a mile off the Tombstone-Tucson road where Milt O'Hara disappeared in May.'

Old Man Clayton exchanged looks with Curly Max. Both men nodded. Then Clem looked at his son Walt and jerked a thumb toward the corral. Walt seemed to know what he meant. He got up and walked to the corral where he roped a horse. Thirty minutes later, rifle asaddle, he was riding toward the Whetstones. Walt Clayton was the best rifle shot in the family. Whenever an assignment of accurate sniping was needed, it was usually given to Walt.

\* \* \*

In an opposite direction from the Whetstones, at the L Bar ranch on Cienega Creek, Ward Larabee raised a floor board and took a bulky package from under it. Until now it had seemed safe enough here. He'd considered himself well above suspicion and his highly respectable ranch house in no danger of being searched.

Now it was different. He'd been on pins and needles ever since Arturo Casteñada had asked him where he was on the morning of Monday, August thirteenth. It was true that the inquiry had been reluctant and apologetic, and that Larabee's answer had quite satisfied Arturo. And yet . . .

There was that kid cousin of Arturo's at the Silva school. She claimed to have seen his face twice, each time from a dark upper window. Once at Calabasas and once at the Tucson school. It could have been while he was calling for Judy Callahan in a carriage. Arturo had clearly derided the whole thing, had even scolded his cousin and made her promise not to mention again what could only be a fantastic illusion. From that quarter there was probably no further danger.

Still, now that the thing had come up it would be risky to leave the Benson loot under a ranch house floor. Others might not be so trusting and gullible as Arturo. If they should hear about the girl's suspicion they might come snooping this way.

A safer hiding place must be found at once. The shift should be made today because tomorrow Larabee's Mexican help would return from the *fiesta*.

With the money in a tin bread box he went to the barn. There he saddled up, tying both the money box and a spade back of his cantle. Then he rode upcreek to select a hiding place well away from his house.

It was three miles up the Cienega to the Callahan ranch and halfway there Larabee came to a spring seeping from the creek bank. It made a good landmark and he decided to use it. Leaving the creek bed he rode to a dwarf cedar about forty yards to the west.

Upslope from the cedar were mixed growths of saguaro, prickly pear, ocotillo, mesquite, and greasewood. Larabee rode well up among them and dismounted at a giant saguaro, sometimes called sentinel cactus.

After pacing fifteen steps upslope from it he dug a hole and buried the money box. After refilling the hole he carefully resodded the spot.

Yet any one of these saguaros looked so much like another that he himself might later be unable to find the right one again. So he took paper and pencil from his pocket and made an accurate, fool-proof sketch. Walking back to the creek he led his horse, counting steps from one landmark to another and jotting the figures down. When he reached the creek bed his sketch was complete.

He folded the sketch and put it in his wallet. Using it as a guide he could return here weeks or months from now, when everything was safe, and quickly find his cache. Should anyone search his house they'd find nothing at all.

★   ★   ★

When the next early morning train pulled in to Tucson from the east, Arturo

Casteñada was on it with a prisoner. He hustled the man into a hack and was driven to the courthouse jail.

Later Sheriff Shibell listened gravely to his report. He counted the nineteen hundred dollars found on Ubrecht and put it in a safe. Presumably it was money stolen from Milton O'Hara. If a court should so judge, in the end it would be given to Milton's only relative and heir, Lynn O'Hara. Ubrecht's body had been left at Benson for burial. 'And Señor Whorton,' Arturo further reported, 'is still at the Dawson place searching for hidden money. Lynn O'Hara has gone to an abandoned mine in the Whetstones.'

'If he finds a body there,' Shibell said grimly, 'we'll have something to work on. Ubrecht wouldn't say who helped him on that stick-up?'

'No, señor. And there is no reason to believe it was our prisoner Dawson. This Dawson insists he did not know Ubrecht was a criminal.'

'If Dawson sticks to it,' the sheriff admitted, 'we'll have no solid case against him.' All we can do is hold him in jail a few days and then turn him loose. Soon as O'Hara gets back, you and he and Whorton better keep on with your mission. I mean you can mosey on to Tombstone and Charlston and see if anybody's been spending those tens with known numbers.'

★　★　★

At a lonely mine in the Whetstones Lynn O'Hara found what he'd dreaded to find — and yet what he'd known all along he must find in the end. Nothing else could be hoped for. The two robbers would surely hide a victim's body where it could not readily be discovered.

The *Vulcan* shaft had a winch. It squeaked on a rusty spindle as Lynn made his Indian guide lower him into it. The second time he went down he took a blanket with him. When he came up he brought along, wrapped in the blanket, a man who'd been dead more than three months.

'We shall take him to town for burial, Cholo.' Lynn's face was gray with bitterness as he helped the Indian load what was left of his brother on the pack mule.

It was just a mile off the Tombstone-to-Tucson stage road and they were mounting to ride there when the shot came.

It seemed to come from a brush hilltop about two hundred yards away and the bullet only missed Lynn by inches. He snatched his own rifle from its scabbard and crouched behind the winch frame, aiming at the brushy hilltop and ready to shoot back at the next puff or flash.

For ten minutes he waited there but the sniper didn't fire again. 'He figured on a one-shot job, Cholo. Betcha he's high tailin' away from here by now. Let's you and I hit for town.'

Again they mounted and Lynn took the mules lead rope. Solemnly they travelled a rutty branch trail to the stage road and on this turned northwest toward the county seat, forty-odd miles away. 'Take us all day and tomorrow, Cholo.'

Tomorrow, Lynn remembered as he rode along, would be Friday again; exactly a week after he'd danced with Judy Callahan.

# 14

Of Tucson's two weekly papers, the *Star* came out on Thursday and the *Citizen* on Saturday. So only the *Citizen* was able to print the news of Lynn's Saturday arrival with the body of a long lost brother.

'The funeral service of Milton O'Hara,' the *Citizen* reported, 'will be held Monday morning at the San Augustine Church, followed by interment at the cemetery on Stone Avenue, just north of Alameda.'

At the Silva school, Judy Callahan read the item and showed it to her roommate.

'I feel awfully sorry for Lynn O'Hara, Gracie. He's a stranger and nearly a thousand miles from home. It says that the brother was his only relative. Now he has no one at all.'

'I too am sad for him,' Altagracia murmured. 'To come all the way here and then find that his brother has been dead for months at the bottom of a mine!

Now he must be laid away in a strange land. A few of the curious will be there I suppose. But no one else. Señor Lynn O'Hara has not been here long enough to have friends.'

'Except us' Judy corrected. 'I met him at a party. You and your father met him at Calabasas. And there's your cousin Arturo; and Roger Niles of the newspaper.'

She looked again at the news item. It mentioned that Arturo Casteñada and Roger Niles, along with four constables borrowed from Ike Brokow's force, would act as pall bearers.

The only real mourner, it seemed to Judy would be Lynn himself.

'I wonder if Miss Silva would take us there, Gracie. Shall we ask her? Perhaps he would feel less lonely if he sees he has sympathy from the few who know him.'

They talked it over and decided that Miss Silva couldn't do worse than say no. And why should she? What could be wrong about chaperoning two girls to a morning church service? Miss Silva

213

listened to them and decided that this wasn't the time to be stern. Theirs was a kindly impulse, and Miss Silva herself was a kindly woman.

★  ★  ★

When on Monday morning she walked her two charges down Convent Street to the Church Plaza, she found the San Augustine sanctuary more than half full of people. However nearly all of them were idlers from the Congress Street and Maiden Lane resorts and were mainly curious to see the Wyoming cowboy who'd shot it out with an Arizona outlaw in a root cellar. According to the latest news sensation, he'd then recovered his murdered brother from a mine shaft at the expense of being sniped at by a hidden rifleman.

Miss Silva and her two girls took seats in the rear pew. At the front a priest stood behind a plain coffin over which he intoned a burial ritual. The most forward bench held the chief mourner but

Judy Callahan could see only the back of his head.

When the service concluded six young men went to the front and picked up the casket. Two were Roger Niles and Arturo Casteñada. The six came solemnly up the aisle bearing the casket, moved past Judy and her companions, and on out to a waiting hearse. Lynn O'Hara followed them out.

Then everyone left the church and when the school group got outside they saw that the hearse and two carriages were ready to leave for the burial ground. One of the carriages held the four borrowed constables. Lynn O'Hara, Roger Niles, and Arturo were about to get into the other.

Then Lynn saw the two young girls and their chaperone standing near the church door. It brought a flush of gratitude to his face. He left the carriage, took off his hat, and walked impulsively to them.

'Thanks for coming. Means a heap to know I've got a few friends. I'm a far piece off my range and feelin' kinda — kinda knotted-up inside. Thanks a lot.' He turned and spoke to Miss Silva. 'Right nice of you to bring them, ma'am.'

The headmistress answered him gravely. 'I could hardly deny them the privilege of comforting a friend.'

'We extend our *consuelos*, Señor O'Hara,' Altagracia murmured formally.

Judy Callahan, usually glib enough, found her tongue tied and said nothing at all.

With a slight bow to them, Lynn turned and went back to his carriage. In a minute the two carriages followed the hearse up Mesilla Street.

Miss Silva led her charges in an opposite direction. 'He has nice manners,' she admitted. 'Your father knows him, Altagracia?'

'But yes, Miss Silva. He came up the *camino real* with us from Calabasas.'

'And you, Judith, have met him only once before?'

'Only once,' Judy said.

'Perhaps,' Altagracia said, 'we shall

never see him again.'

'Who can tell, Gracie?' Judy said it with a disarming innocence. Not even Gracie could be told, yet, that she'd practically made a date with Lynn O'Hara for a week from next Saturday. A week from next Friday afternoon her father would drive her home for a week end at the Circle C and she would persuade Gracie to go along with them. How surprised they must be when two young men named O'Hara and Niles dropped by for a casual call on Mike Callahan!

★   ★   ★

At his courthouse jail Sheriff Shibell grudgingly released a prisoner. 'County Attorney says we can't hold you any longer, Dawson. You were harboring Ubrecht, all right, but we can't prove you knew he was a criminal. So you can go on home now.'

A patient questioning of Joe Dawson had brought no result. Nor had Agent Wally Whorton, after a search of the premises, been able to find any payroll loot at Dawson's San Pedro River place. Whorton was now at Benson waiting to be rejoined there by Lynn O'Hara and Arturo Casteñada. Durango Joe was more than anxious to get away. During the several days he'd spent in jail he'd learned something which must be confided at once to Ward Larabee. Larabee was sitting on a keg of dynamite and didn't know it.

Instead of going by train to Benson, and thence by stage up the San Pedro to his cabin, Durango Joe bought a horse at Tucson and set out by saddle for Larabee's ranch on the Cienega. Larabee had ordered him to stay away but the emergency demanded that the L Bar man be warned without delay.

Joe struck the Cienega at Pantano and rode up it till he sighted the L Bar house. He watched from the brush until after dark when he was sure that the Mexican couple had retired to their own quarters beyond the corral. At the main house a lamp-lighted window indicated that

Ward Larabee was at home.

At Joe's tap, the house door opened and Larabee looked at him angrily. 'I told you to stay away, didn't I? What's the idea . . . ?'

'You'll thank me for coming,' Joe insisted as he slipped in and closed the door. 'Hell's apoppin' Luth.'

'Stop calling me Luth. What's up?'

'They've had me locked up for the last few days,' Joe explained, and I heard talk between the undersheriff and the jailer. A thousand of that Benson money's too hot to handle and we better get shed of it fast!'

Larabee gave him a startled look. 'You mean they've got numbers on it?'

'Only on two packages of fifty tens each,' Dawson said. A thousand dollars in all. The other thirty-one thousand's safe enough. That's why a special agent of the Southern Pacific came here from Frisco. He's lookin' for those tens and if he finds one of 'em in your house you'll land in the pen at Yuma.'

'He won't find anything in my house,

219

Joe. I hid it a long way off.'

Dawson gave a grimace of relief. 'Good! I did the same with my half. Stashed it a piece away from my shack. I remember a package of new tens in it. Other package must be in your half.'

'No doubt it is,' Larabee conceded. He thought the matter over and his eyes narrowed shrewdly. 'You say the Southern Pacific man is out looking for those new tens?'

'Like a bird dog,' Joe said. 'Him and a couple of county deputies. They couldn't find 'em at my place. So now they figger to look for 'em at Tombstone and Charleston. They'll snoop round the gambling tables on a chance someone buys chips with one of those hot tens.'

An idea hit Larabee. He sat nursing it until it took on new angles. 'Look, Joe. The best way to get rid of those hundred hot tens is to plant 'em where they'll sprout wings of innocence for the two of us. Now listen. The main robbery suspects on this range are always the Curly Max-Clem Clayton boys. When they're not raiding, they gamble around Tombstone and Charleston. It wouldn't be hard for you to plant some of the hot money on a couple of 'em.'

Joe's mouth hung open. 'Where would that get us?'

'It would put us in the clear for keeps. They arrest a couple of border gunnies for passing Benson payroll money, and slap em in the Tucson Jail. After which they stop looking for anyone else. They'll be dead sure a couple of Curly Max or Clem Clayton boys pulled the job at Benson.'

The genius of it dawned slowly on Joe. 'It orter work,' he agreed. 'Say I plant a few of those tens on Lucky Luke Bundy at Charleston and a few more on Buckskin Frank Lester at Tombstone. One runs with the Claytons and the other with Curly Max. When they're caught layin' bets with that money, the sheriff figgers he's got the case sewed up.'

'After which, Joe, you and I can breathe easy. Tell you what we'll do. You wait here a couple of hours while I go to my cache. I'll take the hot package out of it and bring it right here. You ride on home with it. In the morning you pick up your own hot package and take both of 'em to Tombstone. Make one plant at Tombstone and another at Charleston.'

'Sounds air tight, Luth. I mean Ward. Do you reckon you can find your cache at night time?'

'It won't be too easy,' Larabee admitted. He moved nearer to the lamp and took a paper from his wallet. Joe Dawson saw him study it for a minute or so. Clearly it was a sketch made to guide Larabee to wherever he'd hidden sixteen thousand dollars.

'Yes, I can find it all right. There's a moon. You wait here till I get back, Joe.'

Larabee went out to the barn. From a house window Joe Dawson watched him saddle a horse and mount with a spade in hand. The spade meant that the money was buried, not hidden in a tree trunk as was Joe's own cache on the San Pedro.

After turning the lamp low Joe lay on a couch and dozed for an hour or so. It was after ten o'clock when he heard Larabee come in. The L Bar man handed him a package of fifty new ten-dollar bills.

'You're right, Joe. The numbers are consecutive. All the rest of the money is old with scattered numbers. Take it and ride.'

Joe Dawson put the package in his coat pocket and went downcreek to the brush patch where he'd left his horse. He could be home by daybreak and pick up a similar package from his hollow tree. After that he'd snatch a little sleep and hit the trail for Tombstone.

From his house door Ward Larabee watched Joe ride east in the moonlight. When he was gone from sight the L Bar man rolled himself a brown paper cigaret and sucked broodingly on it. All the risks were being taken by Joe Dawson. If the Claytons caught him trying to plant the money, they'd make short shift with him. If anything went wrong Joe's life wouldn't be worth a plugged nickel. In one way Broccardi and the Claytons were sensitive. They didn't much mind being accused of a crime they'd really committed. But being accused of one they hadn't committed always made them trigger mad.

What would happen, Larabee pondered, if Durango fouled up his mission and was shot dead by the Charleston crowd? How would anyone ever find the fifteen and a half thousand dollars which Joe had hidden near his cabin on the San Pedro? Would it rot in some badger hole, or hollow snag, or under some rock?

The question intrigued Larabee through three more cigarets. Then the answer came clear and simple. Why let it stay there at all, whether or not Joe failed in his pussy-footing mission? Why couldn't he, Ward Larabee gather it in himself? He could follow Joe to the San Pedro and watch warily from a distance when, just after daybreak tomorrow Joe went to his hiding place to take five hundred dollars from it.

After Joe had ridden on toward Tombstone, Larabee could help himself.

It was too tempting to be resisted. The

L Bar man went to his barn, resaddled his horse and rode east only a few miles in the wake of Durango Joe Dawson.

# 15

Dawn of Tuesday, September fourteenth was just breaking when Ward Larabee tied his mount in a patch of tall mesquite about half a mile west of the San Pedro River. He moved afoot to higher ground where, peering over a greasewood bush, he could see the river bottom and Joe Dawson's cabin on the far bank. He saw Joe's horse in a pole corral and smoke at the cabin chimney. The man couldn't have arrived home more than twenty minutes ago. He'd feed his mount, himself, then snatch a little sleep before visiting his money cache. Naturally he'd avoid having his incriminating package of tens in pocket any longer than necessary.

It was midmorning when Larabee saw Joe come out of his cabin. The man saddled his horse and tied a baggage roll back of the cantle. Larabee watched him ride half a mile up the river and disappear into a small grove of cottonwoods.

It wasn't long before he emerged from the grove and continued on upriver. To Larabee it meant that he'd stopped in the grove to visit a money cache there.

When the man was out of sight Larabee climbed on his horse and rode to the river. He crossed it to the grove and began looking confidently for a hollow tree or snag. There'd been no spade on Joe's saddle, so the man hadn't needed to dig in the ground.

There was a storm-struck snag with an open rift about eight feet above its base. Fresh hoof marks in the sand showed that Dawson had stopped his horse by it. The absence of bootprints meant that the man hadn't dismounted. Probably he'd stood upright on his saddle to reach a hand into the rift.

Ward Larabee did the same and his fingers touched a tightly rolled slicker. He brought it out and knew before he opened it what he'd find. He twisted a cigaret, hooked a leg around his saddle horn and unrolled the slicker. When he counted the money he found it all there. All except what Durango Joe had just taken out of it — a package of fifty new tens. Here were fifteen thousand five hundred dollars robbed from a paymaster at Benson just two weeks ago.

Larabee stuffed the empty slicker back into the snag hole and rode out of the grove. After fording the river he took a bee line for home. Dawson might never learn he'd been robbed. Something violent could happen to him at Charleston or Tombstone. It was certain to happen if Curly Max or the Claytons caught him planting guilty money on one of their men. In which case there'd be no one left who could revisit Joe's cache.

The Southern Pacific's special agent had already spent two days looking for it and had given up.

It was a five-hour ride from the San Pedro to Cienega Creek and the sun was low in the west when Larabee sighted his own tree line. He veered left in order to strike it a mile and a half above his house — at a spring which seeped from the creek bank.

After dismounting at the spring he paced thirty-eight steps beyond it to a cedar tree. Upslope from the cedar there was so much desert vegetation — saguaro, ocotillo and mesquite — that he might have been confused except for a sketch in his wallet. Larabee took it out and held it in hand as he paced twenty-eight steps to a tall ocotillo plant, flowered yellow now in early fall. From there he paced to four other landmarks as the guide sketch indicated, coming out at a giant saguaro. Fifteen paces upslope from this he saw spade marks of his visit last night.

In the dim night light he'd done an insufficient job of resodding and for that reason he'd left his spade hidden in a nearby greasewood bush in order to use it today for a more effective concealment. Now he took the spade and again unearthed a tin box. When he'd slipped the Dawson money into the box it held a treasure of thirty-one thousand dollars, none of which could be identified as part of the Benson loot.

After reburying the box, Ward Larabee took his time at a job of resodding. When he left the place there was nothing to indicate his visit. He need never come back again until the railroad's special agent returned to San Francisco with empty hands, and the hue and cry was cold.

★ ★ ★

When the train from Tucson stopped at Benson that same midnight, Lynn O'Hara and Arturo Casteñada were on it. Wally Whorton was waiting for them on the platform.

'Shibell wired me you were coming, boys. They've just finished what passes for a hotel here and I've booked a room for you.'

'What about our horses?' Lynn asked. Yesterday he'd sent his roan here by train in order to be ready for a ride to Tombstone. Arturo had left his mount here last week before entraining for

Tucson with a prisoner.

'They're grained and ready for the trail,' Whorton said.

The three men walked upstreet to a pine board hotel. When Arturo was out of hearing Lynn spoke in confidence to Whorton. 'When we get to Tombstone let's keep our eyes open for an old prospector named Packsaddle Jones. He's pecking rock in Dragoons and chances are he supplies himself at Tombstone.'

'What do you want to see him for, O'Hara?'

'Want to check out an alibi with him. Likely it's okay; but I want to make sure.'

After six hours of sleep and a fast breakfast they were on their way. They followed upriver along the Benson-Tombstone stage road over which fortunes in silver bullion were moving these days. Late morning brought them to the Dawson place and they found it deserted. 'Shibell turned him loose Monday morning,' Lynn remembered. 'If he rode straight home he could have spent Monday night here.' Today was

Wednesday the fifteenth.

'Somebody was here,' Whorton concluded. 'When I left, the corral gate was closed. Now it's open.'

'Joe could've come home and then headed for the bright lights of Tombstone,' Lynn surmised. 'He'd need a little fun after a weekend in jail.'

They rode on and soon were met and passed by a bullion coach heading for the railroad. The Wells Fargo messenger seated by the driver waved his shotgun at them. Arturo returned the salute. 'He is Morgan Earp of tombstone,' the deputy said. 'Always he rides shotgun for the big silver shipments.'

'Wyatt Earp's brother?' Whorton asked.

'That is right, señor. There are four brothers: Wyatt, Virgil, Morgan, and Warren.' In a moment Arturo added: 'Not long ago Shibell appointed Wyatt as a deputy shriff for the Tombstone section of the county. Now he thinks perhaps he has made a mistake.'

'A mistake?' Lynn queried.

Casteñada shrugged and made a non-committal gesture; and Lynn remembered something about a feud the Earp brothers were carrying on against certain personal enemies around Tombstone; there'd been charges that Wyatt Earp was using his deputy badge to bully his enemies into submission.

'He treated me all right when I was there a month ago,' Lynn said. 'Gave me a list of names and it led me to Ubrecht.'

They rode on and early afternoon brought them to the new smelter town of Contention. Its street was full of mill hands and miners. Lynn knew that his brother Milton had passed through here early on the last morning of his life, riding from Tombstone toward the Whetstones on the stage road to Tucson.

A pick and shovel man with a pair of laden burros had just resupplied himself at a general store. 'That wouldn't be Packsaddle Jones would it?' Lynn asked Arturo.

The Spanish deputy shook his head. 'Packsaddle Jones is an older man with a flowing white beard. If he's prospecting in the Dragoons his closest store would be at Tombstone. You have fatigue, Señor Whorton? Shall we stop here for the night?'

The California man ached in every joint but wouldnt admit it. 'Let's push on to Tombstone.'

They left the river and turned east. In two more hours they sighted Tombstone, miracle town of the Southwest: Eighteen months ago there'd been nothing here but cacti and mesquite. Now there was a city growing so fast that it was about to overtake Tucson in population. By the end of the year it was certain to become the largest city in Arizona.

Its wide streets flanked with high board walks, were lined with crowded stores, saloons, gambling houses, two banks and a theater; hotels of brick, frame and adobe. Ore carts, freight wagons, jack trains and saddle horses filled every hitchrail and most of the men in charge of them wore holster guns. Honkytonk music blared from a dozen doorways along with the shrill laughter of women and a clink of chips.

They rode up Allen Street past the Oriental and Alhambra saloons, stopping at the Occidental Hotel. When they went in to register, Lynn glanced through a doorway into the hotel's bar. A man who stood breasting it had a familiar look.

Lynn gave a nod in that direction. 'I guessed right Arturo. There he is; our friend Joe Dawson.'

It didn't take long to get oriented on the violent political cross-currents operating in and around Tombstone. Two factions were ready to spring at each other's throats with no holds or triggers barred. One was generally known as the Earp faction with its command post at the Oriental Saloon in which Wyatt Earp himself owned a half interest. The other clique centered around Dave Rickenbaugh's Alhambra where Buckskin Frank Lester was chief bartender. Miners generally favored the Oriental; outlaws and near outlaws who called themselves 'cowboys' usually patronized the Alhambra. Of the two Tombstone newspapers, the *Nugget* was backing the Alhambra faction; while the *Epitaph* consistently supported the Earp brothers. Leading enemies of the Earps included Johnnie Behan who planned to run for sheriff against Wyatt Earp whenever a new county was sliced off the east end of Pima County and Tombstone became its county seat.

It was Behan's boast that he could count on solid support from Curly Max and Old Man Clayton, and from the sixty or more 'cowboys' who rode with them.

'But the Earps,' a stage driver named Bud Philpotts confided to Lynn, 'ain't what you'd call lily white themselves. They're all professional gamblers along with that cold-blooded Doc Holliday who sides 'em with a sawed-off shotgun every time they need help.'

'I passed one of 'em on the road today' Lynn remembered. 'Morgan Earp. He's a Wells Fargo messenger on the Benson run.'

Philpotts drooped an eyelid. 'Sure he is. And when he gets to Benson he lays over a couple of days before making the run back to Tombstone. And what does he do at Benson? He caps for the Ed Burns' Top-and-Bottom gang in a saloon there. Makes freeze-out bets for 'em to trim suckers. Morg can deal from both sides of the deck with the best of 'em. The same thing goes on right here in Tombstone.'

Lynn talked it over with Arturo and Whorton.

'Be that as it may,' Whorton concluded, 'our own cue is to throw in with Wyatt Earp. He's a county deputy and knows the ropes here.'

'I have arranged for us to see him tonight,' Arturo said, 'at the Oriental.'

Just after dark they walked down Allen Street, turning in at Tombstone's most popular gambling resort and bar. Every type of card and wheel and dice game was going on under hanging brass lamps which glittered with crystal bangles. Customers stood two deep at a long rosewood bar.

Wyatt Earp himself, half owner of the place, met them just inside the door. He had a long face and massive chin, deep-set blue eyes and tawny mustaches. A cold man, balanced and calm, with a black-butted gun at his hip.

He remembered Lynn from a month ago. 'They tell me you ran down Ubrecht, O'Hara. Was that list of names I gave you any help?'

'Without it,' Lynn admitted, 'I wouldn't have found him.'

Wyatt took them to a stud table and introduced them to his brother Virgil who was dealing there. Virgil, like all the Earp brothers, was a tawny blond. 'Virg figures to run for city marshal against Ben Sippy,' Wyatt announced, 'in the November election. One thing you can bet on; all the hoodlums and horse thieves'll vote against Virg. The crooks around here've got it in for the Earp boys.'

Next Wyatt led them to a faro layout where they met his brother Warren. And to the bar where he set up drinks on the house and introduced them to a thin, ash-blond man whose pale, emaciated face marked him as a consumptive. The man was fastidiously dressed and his name was Holliday. The coldest killer in Arizona, men called him.

'Come on back to my office, Doc,' Wyatt Earp invited. 'These Tucson boys want to let us in on something.'

In a private office at the rear Wally Whorton handed them two lists of numbers. The numbers were consecutive, fifty in each group. 'New ten-dollar bills,' Whorton explained, 'and part of the payroll loot which two men grabbed at Benson two weeks ago. A fair guess is that the two robbers hang out either here or at Charleston. They'll be spending tens. We'd like to catch them at it and pick 'em up.'

The mission suited Wyatt exactly. It could be a chance to move against his own personal enemies, the Curly Max-Clem Clayton coterie of outlaw cowboys. 'What do you want us to do, Whorton?'

'As a county deputy,' the Southern Pacific man suggested, 'you can go quietly to every saloon, restaurant, and livery stable in town. Ask to see the money in their tills on the pretense that you're looking for some counterfeit bills reported in circulation. Really you're looking for the new tens stolen at Benson. If you see one of them, try to find out who spent it.'

'Will do,' Earp agreed vigorously. 'I'll check at the Bird Cage Theater too. They pull in a lot of money with a hot leg show there. Meantime you boys better cover the Alhambra and the Crystal Palace yourselves. They're my main competitors and I wouldn't get much cooperation if I went snooping there. The Alhambra's your best bet. Every outlaw between the Dragoons and the border plays cards there. If you keep your eyes open you might see one of those listed tens tossed on a dice table.'

Whorton looked from Arturo to Lynn and all three men nodded. 'We shall begin tonight,' Arturo decided. 'Señor Whorton, if you will take the Crystal Palace, Lynn and I will take the Alhambra.'

# 16

The Alhambra was a little more crowded and a little noisier than the Oriental. There were fewer miners and more saddle men. The boots under its gaming tables had spurs on them instead of hobnails. Neither place had any female entertainers although Dutch Annie's notorious resort was conveniently across an alley from the Alhambra. The games were the same, except that in addition to card, wheel and dice games the Alhambra also offered a standard pool table where, as Lynn and Arturo entered the place, three shirt sleeved men were playing Call-shot for side bets.

A local constable named Westfall had been sent along by Wyatt Earp to point out certain likely customers.

'That fancy Dan tendin' bar,' Westfall whispered to Lynn and Arturo, 'is Buckskin Frank Lester. Always wears a fringe on his jacket and pants. Not long ago he killed Mickey Glenn, bartender at the Crystal Palace, and then married his widow. Frank's a close friend of Curly Max Broccardi.'

'Is Curly Max himself here?' Lynn asked.

Nope. Curly goes on a bender here sometimes. But he does most of his gambling at Galeyville or Charleston. When he's not gamblmg or stealing steers, he's likely to be lapping up beer at Clem Clayton's ranch on the Pedro.'

'Could Curly have been one of the two Benson payroll robbers?'

'Not a chance. That night Curly Max and Johnnie Ringo were right here in Tombstone on a big drunk. They wrecked a bar on Tough Nut Street and Judge Spicer slapped a fine on 'em.'

'Who's that man with a green eye-shade dealing Faro?

'Professional gambler named Luke Short. He shot and killed Charlie Storms at the Oriental and got a self-defense acquittal. Since then he's done his card riffling over here at the Alhambra.'

In turn Constable Westfall pointed out others of the same hard-case stripe. All were gunslung: Dave Queen; Napa Dick; Jack Madden; Jerry Barton. 'They've all ridden with Curly Max or the Claytons at one time or another. Most any of 'em could've been in on the Benson job.'

'Look, *amigo*!' Arturo nudged Lynn and spoke in an undertone. 'Is not that José Dawson?' He pointed toward a pool table at the rear.

One of the three shirt-sleeved pool players was indeed Durango Joe Dawson, only a few days ago released from the Tucson jail. Lynn had seen him earlier at the Occidental Hotel bar. 'Who are the men with him, Constable?'

Westfall took a good look. 'They are Dutchy Tyler and Zwing Hunter. Both of them have served time at Yuma. We think both of them were in on the Fronteras massacre across the border but we can't prove it. Zwing Hunter lives at Galeyville. They say he's second in command there and stands ace high with Curly Max.'

'What did he serve time for?'

'Stage robbing.'

Lynn moved curiously nearer to the pool table and watched the three pool players mainly because Durango Joe was one of them. He couldn't forget that Durango had given shelter to one of two men who'd killed Milton O'Hara. It was a hot night and all three pool players, after shedding coats, had rolled their shirt sleeves above the elbows. Lynn saw Joe Dawson miss a shot and then stand back to chalk his cue.

It was Dutchy Tyler's turn and he ran six balls, calling each shot in advance. Zwing Hunter, who'd served time for stage robbing, stood waiting his turn. Absently Lynn noticed that Joe Dawson stood near a wall rack where three coats were hanging. Presumably one of the coats was his own because he took a match from it and lighted a cigaret.

The game ended with Tyler winning. Dawson and Hunter each paid him a dollar and the balls were racked for another game. Not much chance of a ten-dollar bill changing hands here, Lynn concluded, so he crossed the room to stand near a counter where a house man was selling chips. There he watched to see if anyone bought chips with a new ten-dollar bill.

No one did. Nor did anyone drop a new ten on a dice or poker table. Arturo spent the evening circulating the room, occasionally participating in a game. Wally Whorton no doubt was doing the same at the Crystal Palace.

An hour after midnight they gave it up.

'It's a long shot,' Whorton admitted when Lynn and Arturo joined him at their hotel. 'Maybe the robbers noticed those new tens with consecutive numbers and got leery. In that case they'd be careful not to spend them for a long long time.'

'Or maybe they didn't come to Tombstone. They could be finding their fun at Charleston or Harshaw or Galeyville.'

'*Mañana*,' Arturo said patiently, 'we will try again.'

In the morning they checked with Wyatt Earp who reported no luck so far. He'd given the two lists of numbers to every shop and hotel keeper he could trust asking them to watch for an incriminating ten. 'Maybe the two guys are still lying low in the hills,' he said. 'Maybe they'll show up tomorrow.'

If the guilty men showed up in Tombstone the next day they apparently didn't spend one of the incriminating tens. From the time the Alhambra opened its games at noon until long past midnight Lynn and Arturo kept an eye on whatever currency changed hands there. Whorton did the same at the Crystal Palace while Virgil Earp checked incoming currency at the Oriental. Wyatt Earp kept in close touch with the local bankers who would inspect all ten-dollar bills brought in for deposit.

Again a long evening went by and again the watch netted nothing.

'So tomorrow's another day,' Whorton said doggedly.

'I didn't see Joe Dawson around

today,' Lynn remarked. 'Maybe he left town.'

Friday morning the seventeenth Lynn slept late at his hotel. While most of the Tombstone bars kept open around the clock, the gambling tables were shut down till noon. The town was relatively quiet when at half past nine Lynn strolled to a livery stable for a look at his horse.

The roan had been idling in a stall for forty hours and needed exercise. So Lynn saddled up for a brisk canter through the streets of the town. 'Be back in half an hour,' he told the barnman.

The horse was full of life and needed no spurring as Lynn made it kick dust up Allen Street. He rode by the O.K. corral and at Fourth Street passed Hafford's saloon where a freighter was unloading kegs of beer. At Fifth he passed the *Epitaph* office and a door farther on saw Ed Schiefflin, who'd made the first silver strike here and who was already a millionaire, come out of Brown's Hotel with Judge Spicer. Schiefflin Hall and the Oriental Saloon were in that same block.

At this early hour most of the hitchrails were empty.

Lynn O'Hara rode on, straight in the saddle and gunslung at the hip. His saddle scabbard still had his carbine in it. At the Bird Cage Theater he turned right to Tough Nut Street where he veered back west, again riding the full length of the town. He rode past the *Nugget* office and Charlie Tarbell's Eagle Hotel, and on between rows of false-fronted shops. At Fifth and Tough Nut a woman was sweeping off her walk. She'd been pointed out to Lynn as Nellie Cushman — a generous woman who ran the Russ House and whom men called 'Angel of the Camp.' Any penniless prospector could always find food and lodging at Nellie Cushman's.

She raised a hand and stopped Lynn with a question. 'Have you found it yet, young man? I know what you're looking for. Wyatt Earp gave me a list of numbers.'

'No luck yet. Thanks, Mrs. Cushman.'
At the foot of Tough Nut Lynn veered

over to Fremont Street and again rode the length of the town. Two men were pitching horse shoes in front of a blacksmith shop and they waved a salute as Lynn passed. He knew them as Sherman McMasters and Jack Vermillion, one a lookout and the other a dealer at the Oriental. According to Constable Westfall they were stalwarts in the Earp faction and deadly enemies of the so-called cowboy faction.

Allen Street was still quiet when Lynn got back to his livery stable. As he dismounted in front of it an excited liveryman came running out with a ten-dollar bill in his hand. 'Where's Wyatt Earp? Better round him up quick, O'Hara. Look what a man just paid his barn bill with!'

Lynn took the ten-dollar note and read the number on it. It was one of the listed numbers and therefore part of the Benson payroll loot. 'Who gave you this?' he asked sharply.

'It was Zwino Hunter. He owed me eight dollars and I gave him two bucks change. Didn't notice the number till you rode up just now. Zwing took his horse and hit the trail for home.' The liveryman pointed east up Allen Street. He lives at Galeyville and that's a fur piece from here.'

'How long's he been gone?'

'Not more'n twenty minutes. Wyatt could easy ketch up with him on a good horse. Better fetch him here right away.'

'I'll handle it myself.' But first Lynn took the man into the barn office where he dipped pen into ink. He made the man scratch his initials on a corner of the bill. 'So you can identify it in court. Now take it to Wally Whorton and Deputy Casteñada at the Occidental Hotel. If they're still asleep, wake 'em up. Tell 'em I'm off after Zwing Hunter.'

Again Lynn rode the length of Allen Street and this time he used spurs. The roan was at a hard run when they hit the trail to Galeyville which lay some forty miles east, almost to the New Mexico line, on Turkey Creek in the Chiricahuas. The forbidding Chiricahuas, long known as a stronghold for outlaws and warring Apaches!

A mile out of Tombstone the desert closed about Lynn, the grim Dragoons to his left and the piñon-studded Mule Mountains on his right. To save wind for his horse he slowed to a trot. Zwing Hunter didn't know he was being followed. So he'd have no reason to hurry. A stage robber and a crony of Curly Max! The Benson payroll job fit his talents, all right. What else had Westfall said about him? That he'd probably taken part in the Fronteras massacre across the border. Which would make him one of Don Vicente's *sin verguenzas*. The shameless ones!

A twenty minute start would put him not more than two miles ahead. And about six miles out of Tombstone, after topping a rise, Lynn sighted a rider.

The man was jogging leisurely east in the direction of Chiricahua Peak. Galeyville lay in a gulch just south of that peak, highest and most remote in all of Pima County. A wild country where many a renegade, both Apache and white, had for years eluded the law. That, Lynn knew, was why a move was on foot to make a new county out of this region, so that a sheriff could be based at Tombstone.

The man ahead rode a brown pony and Lynn, spurring again to a lope, rapidly gained on him. Presently the man dipped out of sight into an arroyo. When he didn't reappear on the other side, Lynn knew that he'd become aware of pursuit and was waiting under cover.

A hundred yards from the arroyo Lynn saw the glint of sunlight on a rifle barrel. Zwing Hunter was an experienced fugitive and knew all the tricks. *He's got a bead on me right now!* Lynn thought as he stepped quickly from the saddle.

Here the greasewood was five feet high and when he was on foot in a crouch it hid Lynn from the arroyo. He tied his horse to a bush, took the carbine from its scabbard and advanced warily.

A covey of quail whirred away and went sailing across the arroyo. Lynn waited a minute and then moved on in a crouch. Angling to the left he struck the arroyo about fifty yards below the trail. From its rim there he could see Zwino Hunter. The man had flattened himself on the arroyo slope with only his head and hat and rifle showing above the bank. He was aiming down the trail, ready for whoever followed him.

Lynn whipped his carbine stock to cheek and drew a bead of his own. Holding it, he advanced slowly along the arroyo's rim. He'd cut the distance in half before Hunter saw him.

'I'm a county deputy,' Lynn shouted, 'and you're under arrest.'

The Galeyville man whipped around on his knees, swinging his rifle barrel this way. But he didn't fire and Lynn took five or six more steps toward him.

'The law wants you, Zwing Hunter.'

'What for?'

'For snatching a payroll at Benson. Drop your rifle and turn your back this way.'

To Lynn's surprise the man did just

that. He dropped the rifle, stood up and turned his back toward Lynn O'Hara. In that pose he said sullenly: 'You've got the wrong man, mister. I wasn't on that Benson Job.'

'You just paid a livery bill with part of the take.' Lynn took another step and as he closed the gap it looked like an easy arrest.

All at once he learned better. Zwing Hunter had dropped his rifle but his thigh holster still had a six-gun in it. He drew and spun about, firing twice.

Lynn felt the breath of both bullets. He let loose a bullet of his own and its impact brought a yell from the man. The Galeyville outlaw clutched at his ribs and went down from a hit just above the belt buckle. He sank to the sand and went sliding down the slope to lay groaning on the bed of the wash.

# 17

Three hard-riding horsemen came pounding the trail from Tombstone. Arturo Casteñada, Wally Whorton, and Wyatt Earp emerged from a cloud of dust and drew rein at the arroyo. Looking down into it they saw Zwing Hunter on his back in the sand with Lynn O'Hara kneeling by him.

'He was lucky,' Lynn reported. 'Bullet went between two ribs and I've got the bleeding stopped.' Always he carried a first aid bandage in his saddlebag and he'd used it promptly on Hunter.

'You got the right man, all right,' Whorton assured him. 'The number on that bill checks with the list. Want to tell us who your pard was, Hunter?'

The Galeyville man cursed him. 'Get me to a doctor, damn you!'

Later as they were taking him to Tombstone, he swore he'd never been in Benson in his life. If he had a piece of stolen money in his pocket he must have won it at cards or dice in Tombstone. 'I was in Mexico the night that payroll was snatched.'

'What doing?' Wyatt Earp prodded. 'Stealing cattle? And who was with you?'

For that Zwing Hunter had no answer.

Riding collapsed over a saddle horn for six miles put him in a faint by the time they got him to a cell cot. Doctor George Goodfellow treated him there and made a favorable report. 'He'll live to hang, boys. The slug didn't touch anything but flesh. Went through clean as a whistle. Just feed him and keep him quiet.'

The lawmen spent most of the afternoon trying to coax from Zwing Hunter the name of his partner in the Benson hold-up. 'Did you split the take? What did you do with your cut, Zwing?'

'I wasn't there, blast you!' It was all they could get out of the man.

But Wyatt Earp had a firm idea about it. 'I'll bet my saddle the other guy was Billy Grounds. They've pulled more than one stage job together, that pair. Always got off except once when Zwing couldn't promote himself a fake alibi. The Benson payroll job fits them like a glove.'

'Where,' Lynn asked, 'could we find Billy Grounds?'

'In Charleston. He keeps a permanent room at the Flores House there. Spends half his time shooting craps and the other half cowboying with the Clayton bunch upriver.'

'So let's get a search warrant,' Wally Whorton proposed, 'and see what we can find in that room at the Flores House.'

Judge Spicer issued the search warrant. 'Virgil and I'd better go along with you,' Wyatt Earp decided. 'Won't hurt to take Doc Holliday along too. Charleston's crawling with Billy Grounds' friends and those fellas stick together. Might take five or six of us to make an arrest.'

Early on the morning of Saturday, September eighteenth, six riders took the Charleston road out of Tombstone. O'Hara, Casteñada, Whorton, Wyatt and Virgil Earp, and a thin, pale consumptive with a short shotgun on his saddle. The distance was twelve miles with McCann's Last Chance saloon at the halfway point. As they rode by the Last Chance without stopping McCann called curiously from his doorway: 'What's up, Wyatt? You got the deadwood on somebody?'

'Let you know later,' Earp said as they rode on.

It was much the same when they passed the old Bronkow mine down the road. Again the six men evaded curious questions and rode on. In midmorning they jogged into the dusty street of what some called the roughest outlaw town in the Southwest, with the possible exception of Galeyville. 'Six hundred people here,' Wyatt Earp told Lynn. 'About a third of 'em are smelter hands; another third are in the saloon and dice business; another third call themselves cowboys and steal stock for a living.'

'Birds like Jerry Barton there.' Virgil Earp nodded toward a two-gunned loafer rigged out in a flannel shirt and cowboy chaps who sat perched on the hitchrail at Schwartz's saloon.

'Brags he's killed seventeen men, Jerry does, and I wouldn't put it past him.'

Half a block on they came to the meat shop of Jim Burnett. Burnett gave an oily smile as the six riders came abreast. 'I'm not picking you up this time,' Wyatt Earp told him. To Lynn he explained: 'He's been in court twice for peddling stolen beef to the mines. Both times he got off by showing a forged bill-of-sale. Hand-in-glove with the Claytons, Jim is.'

'I see we've got two friends in town,' Virgil Earp said. 'Hello, Mac; howdy, Mr. Schneider.' They stopped for a word with two men who stood on the walk in front of Ohnesorgen's stage depot. Arturo already knew them. Virgil Earp presented them to Lynn and Whorton. 'McKelvey's the constable here, Lynn. Mr. Schneider's chief engineer at the smelter. Had any more trouble with Johnnie-behind-the-Deuce, Mr. Schneider?'

The engineer shrugged. 'Nothing but a little sass. That tin-horn's all talk.'

'He's got a weak mind and an itchy trigger finger,' Wyatt warned. 'He's the kind who'd shoot a man just to show off. Are the Clayton boys in town, McKelvey?'

The constable shook his head. 'They're all out at the ranch today. Curly Max Broccardi's payin' 'em a visit, I hear. So's Lucky Luke Bundy and a few other upstanding horse thieves.'

'What about Billy Grounds?'

'He's in town. Saw him go into the Schwartz bar a while ago.'

The six men from Tombstone rode on to the Flores House and dismounted. In the lobby they found the proprietor, Antonio Flores, watering a pot of geraniums. Lynn looked into the dining room and saw Durango Joe Dawson dawdling over a cup of Coffee. It could be a late breakfast or an early lunch. 'That fella sure gets around,' Lynn said. 'Saw him Wednesday night playing pool at the Alhambra.'

'Might be on his way to the Clayton ranch,' Virgil guessed. 'He used to ride with that bunch.'

Wyatt Earp accosted the proprietor. 'Billy Grounds keeps a room here. We've a warrant to search it. Take us up there and let us in.'

Antonio Flores gaped for a moment, then gave a shrug of acquiescence. 'As you wish, señor.' He took a key from the key rack and led the way upstairs. There he opened the room of Billy Grounds.

Cowboy trappings were scattered about and the bed hadn't been made. With six men to search it didn't take long.

'Here we are,' Whorton announced jubilantly. He'd dumped the contents of a duffel bag on the floor. At the bottom of the bag was a rolled jacket tied with pigging strings. After unrolling it Wally Whorton exposed a package of new ten-dollar bills with consecutive numbers. 'Just what we're looking for, boys.'

'So let's get over to the Schwartz place,' Wyatt Earp said grimly, 'and pick up Billy Grounds.'

At the Schwartz hitchrail they left Doc Holliday outside to watch the street, in case friends of Billy Grounds should approach to challenge the arrest.

The other five men from Tombstone went in and found six poker players at a table. Three others stood looking on and another trio were drinking at the bar. It was a shabby place with a sawdust floor and untidy box cuspidors. The pine walls were unpainted but decorated with gaudily framed pictures of thinly draped women. The bartender was Chinese. Schwartz himself wasn't in sight.

The Earp brothers knew all the dozen customers by name. 'Hardcases,' Wyatt said to Lynn just inside the door. 'The man dealing cards is Billy Grounds. The men playing with him are Alex Arnett, Mort Hicks, Josh McGill, Chuck Green, and Harry Earnshaw. Stage-robbing killers, all of 'em. The three watching the game are Clayton hands. The little guy at the bar is the one they call Johnnie-behind-the-Deuce. He brags he's gonna shoot holes through Mr. Schneider some day, just for the fun of it. The pair drinking with him are Jerry Barton and Indian Tom. Tom's a scout for Curly Max Broccardi.'

'Will they try to protect Grounds?'

'They might. Odds of twelve to five might look good to 'em.'

It had been decided that Arturo Casteñada, as a regular deputy from the county seat, would make the arrest. 'We'll cover you, Arturo,' Wyatt promised. He motioned Lynn O'Hara to a position left of the poker table while his brother and Whorton took positions to the right of it. Arturo advanced alone to the table and touched Billy Grounds on the shoulder.

'I represent the sheriff of Pima County, señor, and with regret I must arrest you for the stealing of payroll money at Benson.'

Instantly Billy Grounds and all of the five playing with him were on their feet.

Each of them wore a gunbelt and gun. The three at the bar spun around to face Arturo. So did the trio of onlookers at the table. Lynn saw hands creep slowly toward gun butts. There was a breathless moment while twelve men and twelve guns were poised to contest the arrest.

Then Wyatt Earp gave a crisp warning. 'Steady there, men. Deputy Casteñada's not by himself. We're here to back him up. Shoot him and you'll have to shoot all of us. The arrest sticks and if you're smart you won't try to stop it.' For another dozen ticks of the barroom clock Lynn O'Hara felt certain they would try to stop it. It showed in their eyes and in a dozen hands crooked for a draw. They were all outlaw comrades of Billy Grounds and sworn enemies of the Earp crowd. At the moment the odds heavily favored them and they were itching to shoot it out.

Then a sudden change came. A thin, black-coated man with a sallow face stepped through the half-doors. He had a sawed-off, Wells Fargo shotgun with both of its triggers cocked. He pointed it at no one. He said nothing. He merely stood there somberly eyeing the room.

Hands that had been creeping toward holsters suddenly went limp. Heads hot for a showdown suddenly cooled off. One look at Doc Holliday and his double-barreled threat of buckshot death took the fight out of them. Harry Earnshaw licked his lips and said hoarsely: 'Well, Billy, maybe you'd better go along with 'em. They can't pin nothin' on you. We can all swear where you was that night — and it was a long way from Benson.'

'Sure, Billy,' Johnnie-behind-the-Deuce chimed in from the bar. 'They can't prove nothin'.'

All resistance melted. Arturo took Grounds by one arm and Whorton took him by the other. The man was led outside and a horse was brought for him. Twenty minutes later he was riding as a prisoner toward Tombstone.

As he rode at the rear with Arturo, Lynn had an uneasy feeling about it.

Somehow the finding of evidence so easily didn't quite convince him. Why hadn't they found some of the unidentifiable money in Grounds' duffel bag? Why would only the incriminating bills turn up in the man's baggage? Had the tens been planted there by someone else?

They'd come within an eyelash of a showdown fight, back there in Charleston. In a shoot-out at least half the men in the room would have been killed. Only the sinister menace of Holliday's shotgun had stopped it. Of that Lynn was certain. Those San Pedro River outlaws were clearly more afraid of Doc Holliday than of all the four Earp brothers combined. Halfway to Tombstone they topped at McCann's Last Chance roadhouse for drinks. McCann leaned across his bar with some advice.

'You caught 'em by surprise, Wyatt. If Clem Clayton's whole crew had been in town they'd've shot it out. Curly Max is at the Clayton place. He's close pards with both Zwing Hunter and Billy Grounds. When they hear of this they'll go roarin' into Tombstone bent on riggin' a jailbreak. That gang's got plenty of friends right in Tombstone who'd side 'em.'

Wyatt Earp was a realist and he knew it was true. The anti-Earp faction would try to discredit the arrests. The *Epitaph* would support him but the *Nugget* would side with his enemies.

'So what do you advise, McCann?'

'Don't try to hold Hunter and Grounds in your Tombstone jail. Slap 'em in a buckboard and race 'em to a train at Benson. From there you can scoot 'em by train to the county jail at Tucson.'

Riding on with the prisoner Wyatt Earp said to Arturo, 'It was good advice and we'd better take it.'

His brother Virgil agreed. 'Not only that, but we'd better take along about ten armed outriders for guards. Be just like Old Man Clayton to come chasin' after us with every gun he can muster.'

Arturo gave a solemn nod. 'Let us do it that way, señores.'

★  ★  ★

At daybreak Sunday, September nineteenth a buckboard rolled out of
Tombstone on the Benson stage road.
Fourteen outriders flanked it. In the
buckboard's bed was a mattress on which
lay the wounded Zwing Hunter. Virgil
Earp was driving with Billy Grounds,
manacled, sitting by him.

The last house in town was a cottage
with a wooden cross on its ridgepole.
Passing it, Lynn saw a few women going
in. Each woman wore a hat or headcloth
and seemed dressed in her best clothes.
He wondered why they'd be out at daybreak. Then he noticed an old man with
a white flowing beard in the act of tying
a burro in front of the cottage. 'Wonder
what's going on, this early,' Lynn said to
Warren Earp who rode beside him. They
were a length or two back of the others.

'Tombstone hasn't got a church yet,'
Warren explained. 'But a priest showed
up and he figures to build one. Meantime he offers to hold early mass at his

house on Sundays.'

And today was Sunday. Lynn rode on another fifty yards and then remembered something. That old prospector, Packsaddle Jones! Arturo had described him as being very religious. In which case he might come all the way from his camp in the Dragoons to attend early mass in Tombstone.

'Be back in a minute,'Lynn said to Warren Earp. He whirled his mount and loped back to the cottage gate. The man with the white flowing beard hadn't yet gone inside. Are you the one they call Packsaddle Jones?'

'That's me, mister. Anything on your mind?'

'Yes. A man said you stopped at his ranch for lunch at noon of Monday, the thirtieth of August. You were travelling east toward the Dragoons with a pair of burrows. It would be two weeks ago last Monday. Do you remember?'

The old man closed his eyes and thought back studiously. 'Sure I remember. It was the L Bar on Cienega Creek.

Ward Larabee took right good care of me. Why?'

'If he was there at that time,' Lynn explained, 'it proves he wasn't somewhere else. By the way, Mr. Jones, where did you stop the night before you got to the L Bar?'

'I camped in the Empire Hills,' the old man said.

'And the day before that you'd travelled from Tucson?'

'No. From the San Xavier mission. I attended mass there. And now, if you'll excuse me I mustn't be late for this one.' Packsaddle Jones turned and went into the cottage.

Lynn spurred down the road to catch up with a buckboard under guard of fourteen men. Each of those guards had a rifle and some of them had shotguns. On this ride Doc Holliday wasn't with them. After yesterday's round trip to Charleston he'd had a relapse and a fit of coughing. Doctor Goodfellow had ordered him to bed.

Wyatt Earp and his two best gunfighters, Sherman McMasters and Jack

Vermillion, dropped back to the rear and looked warily over their shoulders. If the Clayton-Curly Max gang followed bent on a rescue it could be a running fight all the way. 'We're bound to have a showdown with the Claytons some day,' Wyatt predicted, 'but this is not the right time or place. I'd rather stand flat-footed with them on the street at Tombstone; or maybe some day when they're saddling up at the O.K. corral.'

'What I'm leery of,' McMasters pondered, 'is that they'll ride straight down the San Pedro and get ahead of us. They could do that if they started last night. If they're ahead of us, they could drygulch us as we ride by.'

The buckboard party struck the river at Contention and there they turned down the east bank. From here on Lynn rode ahead with Wally Whorton and kept a sharp lookout for ambush signs. Any brush patch or cottonwood grove could hide thirty avenging rifles.

The miles dropped behind them and there was no attack. And by the time they reached Joe Dawson's deserted cabin Lynn felt reasonably sure there'd be none.

'The case is all washed up,' Whorton remarked, 'except for finding out what they did with thirty-one thousand in safe bills. Where would you guess, O'Hara?'

'*Quien sabe?*' Lynn answered absently. His mind was on an old prospector who'd attended a mass in Tombstone this morning, and who'd attended another one two or three weeks ago at the San Xavier mission. Why not inquire of the mission priest and confirm the day Packsaddle Jones had stopped there? It would be exactly one day *before* he'd nooned at the L Bar with Ward Larabee. The prospector, to whom one day would be like any other, might be confused as to just when he'd stopped at a certain ranch. But a mission priest would know exactly when he'd had such a conspicuous worshipper as Packsaddle Jones.

Thinking of dates brought a pleasant matter to Lynn. Six days from now would be Saturday the twenty-fifth — a day when he could be reasonably sure of running into Judy Callahan at her father's ranch.

Cannily his mind scheduled the intervening time. Tonight they'd take the prisoners by train to Tucson, leaving one man to follow by road with the horses.

During the early part of the week there'd be hearings and arraignments. At all of them Lynn O'Hara must stand by as a witness. He'd be needed to help guard the Tucson jail in case of an attempt to rescue Hunter and Grounds. Pressure would be put on Hunter and Grounds to make them tell where they'd hidden thirty-one thousand dollars. Their outlaw friends would also want to know that secret and the only way they could find out would be to rescue the prisoners. They'd plotted a bold rescue before in the case of Gil Stilwell.

But by Friday morning everything should have calmed down and Lynn O'Hara would be due a day off. A Saturday when he could show up innocently at the Circle C and be surprised to find a red-haired girl from the Silva school there. A girl who'd taken a roommate home with her for the week end. Which reminded Lynn that he must bring along Roger Niles too — for a stolen date with Altagracia Casteñada.

# 18

The same Monday morning on which Deputies Casteñada and O'Hara delivered Zwing Hunter and Billy Grounds to the Tucson Jail, Durango Joe Dawson arrived home at his cabin on the San Pedro River. His mission was accomplished and there'd been no hitch. The guilt of a payroll robbery was now solidly planted on two men whose talents and past records happened to fit the job neatly. The pair had been promptly arrested and taken to the county seat.

Smart as a fox, Ward Larabee was, to figure it out like that. The law would still look for the stolen money, but not in the direction of Dawson or Larabee. They'd be sure that Zwing Hunter and Billy Grounds had split the money and that each had buried the bulk of his cut somewhere. There'd be no reason to suspect anyone else.

Joe unsaddled and turned his horse

loose in a small pasture. After feeding himself he napped for a few hours. After that he drank himself drunk from a quart of whiskey he'd brought down river from Charleston.

It was Tuesday morning before he sobered up. He soaked his head in the river and shaved the shagginess from his face. Why not ride to Tucson for a few days in the bright lights? The *fiesta* was over but there was still plenty of fun to be had around Levin's Park or at the *Barrio* cantinas. The law wouldn't bother him. Only a week ago yesterday they'd turned him loose for lack of evidence. He could thumb his nose at the law and have a good time with the *muchachas* on Maiden Lane.

He'd need some spending money. A hundred dollars would do.

To get it Joe Dawson saddled his horse and rode upriver to a cottonwood grove. Before entering it he looked cautiously in all directions. When he was sure that no human was within miles of him, he rode to a cottonwood snag in the grove and stood upright on his saddle.

Reaching into a rift high on the snag Joe brought out a rolled slicker. It seemed thinner and flatter than it should be. When he unrolled it there was nothing inside. Fifteen and a half thousand in currency was gone and the dismal fact brought a hollowness to the pit of Joe Dawson's stomach.

Had the railroad's special agent, Whorton, found and seized the money? No, because in that case he would have stayed here to arrest Joe Dawson. The man had spent two days searching and digging near the cabin. Joe was sure that he'd found nothing at all.

Someone else had found and rifled this cache!

On the ground near the snag Joe saw the snipe of a cigaret. A brown paper cigaret! He remembered that Ward Larabee smoked brown paper cigarets and the truth flashed. It was Larabee who'd taken the money. Larabee who'd told him to take a package of tens from the cache and plant it on some likely outlaw at Tombstone or Charleston!

The bitter truth was clear now. Larabee must have followed him here, at daybreak that morning, and watched from a distance to see Joe ride into the grove. After that it would be simple enough to find the hiding place.

For a while the loss stunned Durango Joe Dawson and left him with a sense of dull helplessness. He rode back to the cabin and poured himself a whisky. The liquor changed his mood from despair to fury. Why should he let Larabee get away with it? Larabee who now had both cuts of the Benson money and no doubt was laughing at him!

*But I've got things on that guy! He's wide open. He'll hand it back to me — or else!*

He, Joe Dawson, could tell tales on Larabee. It couldn't be the tale of Calabasas, where Pancho Morales had been shot dead, because Joe himself had helped with that job. For the same reason it couldn't be the tale of the Benson payroll hold-up.

But it could be a tale of Wichita. He

could go to Larabee and threaten to write an anonymous letter to the sheriff at Wichita, Kansas, giving the whereabouts of Luther Ward Larabee who'd killed a man there five years ago. The Kansas officer would investigate. And while a five-year-old killing by a man in a distant territory might not lead to a conviction, even an inquiry would embarrass Larabee. He was hoping to marry the heiress of a neighboring ranch. If Mike Callahan heard only a breath of talk about a Kansas killing, it would snuff out whatever chance Larabee had at the Circle C.

'I've got him where the wool's short!' Joe took another drink. Then he buckled on a gun and went out to his horse.

He'd ride at once to the L Bar for a showdown. Larabee would have two choices: to come clean with the money or go for his gun. 'But he'll lay off the gunplay,' Joe concluded as he rode west toward the Cienega. Guillermo and Maria Sanchez, the Mexican couple who worked for Larabee, were now at home from the *fiesta* and would be within ear-shot of any gunfire at the ranch house. Killing Dawson, with the Sanchez couple on the premises, would be too stupid a risk for Larabee to take.

'I've got him on the hip!' Durango Joe dug in with his spurs and rode for a showdown with Ward Larabee.

When he got to the L Bar no one was there but Maria Sanchez. 'They are at the roundup, my Guillermo and the *patron*.' She pointed west toward the Empire Hills.

Joe knew that Larabee's small L Bar herd ranged there, sharing a free open range with larger herds belonging to Mike Callahan and Louee Vail. It would be a mixed roundup with the Callahan and Vail crews in command of it. Their shoestring neighbor, Ward Larabee, would be expected to lend a hand or two. Calves missed at the spring roundup would be branded and any beef needed for fall shipment would be cut out. Usually such a roundup waited till October but steers had fattened early this season and there was a tempting market.

'When'll they be back?' Joe asked Maria.

Her husband, she told him, would remain at the roundup camp for another week or so, until the fall work was completed. 'But the *patron*,' she said, 'will come home Saturday morning.'

The delay irked Joe. But there was nothing he could do about it. He couldn't ride to the hills and have a showdown with Larabee in front of the Vail and Callahan crews. Best to see him alone here Saturday morning. 'Thanks, Maria,' Joe wheeled his mount and rode sullenly back toward the San Pedro.

★ ★ ★

At the Tombstone courthouse, after testifying at the preliminary hearings of Zwing Hunter and Billy Grounds, Lynn O'Hara took up a loose end with Arturo Casteñada.

'The last man I saw at Tombstone, Arturo, was your old prospector Packsaddle Jones. I checked the alibi from a friend of yours and it seems to stand up.'

'I knew it would,' Arturo said with a smile. 'My friend is a *caballero* of honor and distinction. My silly little cousin simply made a mistake.'

'More than likely,' Lynn conceded. 'Still, there's one more check I wish you'd make. First chance you get take a ride to the San Xavier mission and talk with the priests there. On the day before he got to the L Bar, Packsaddle attended a mass at San Xavier. If it was a Sunday mass he got to the L Bar on Monday. If he attended a midweek mass, say on a Wednesday, he didn't get to the L Bar till Thursday. In which case Larabee's alibi blows up. Top of that it'd make him a liar and we'd know your cousin told the truth about him after all.'

The Spanish deputy shrugged tolerantly. 'you do not know him as well as I do, my friend. But as you wish. Just to satisfy you I shall speak at the first opportunity with the priests at San Xavier.'

★ ★ ★

Eighty miles to the southeast, again in the shade of a cottonwood back of Old Man Clayton's ranch house, the Claytons and Max Broccardi were glumly pondering an impasse. Two of their heelers were in jail at the county seat charged with a crime of which they couldn't possibly be guilty.

The payroll hold-up at Benson had taken place at 12:05 A.M., September first. 'Which was the same night,' Old Man Clayton protested bitterly, 'when my boys raided Don Juan Elias' beef herd down on the border. Zwing Hunter and Billy Grounds were with 'em. So how the hell could they be stickin' up a payroll at Benson?'

It was clear that the arresting lawmen had made a mistake. Yet how could the Claytons offer Hunter and Grounds an alibi which, if accepted, would involve them and the Claytons in another felony?

Broccardi and Clem Clayton had sweated over it for days. They'd considered forming a rescue party of twenty or more guns and marching on the Tucson jail. On a dark night maybe they could outgun the jailers and set two innocent comrades free. Innocent, that is, of the particular guilt they were charged with.

But the rescue idea, it was decided by Wednesday afternoon, was too risky. Even if it succeeded they'd be sure to lose some men and those who got away would be harried by the law for the rest of their lives.

'But we gotta do something!' Ike Clayton exploded. 'It's a dirty deal, any way you look at it.'

His brothers were no less indignant. They were peculiarly sensitive when charged with crimes committed by persons outside their organization. 'Somebody must've planted that money on Zwing and Billy,' Walt Clayton argued. 'If I knew who it was I'd sure burn him down.'

It was late Thursday before they found out. The informer was the pussy-footing little gambler from Charleston known as Johnnie-behind-the-Deuce.

'It was Joe Dawson!' the Deuce announced breathlessly after a fast ride from town.

'You mean Durango Joe?' Clem Clayton asked sharply. 'What makes you think so?'

'Flossie tipped me.' They knew that Flossie was a chambermaid at the Flores House and that the Deuce kept company with her. 'She seen Joe Dawson sneaking outa Billy Grounds' room. It was just before those deputies showed up at Charleston. He could've planted the package of money in the duffel bag.'

Curly Max asked, 'What about the tenner that Zwing paid his livery bill with at Tombstone?'

The littler gambler drooped a wise eyelid. 'Same answer. Joe Dawson. Dutchy Tyler just rid in from Tombstone. He says him and Zwing and Dawson were playin' pool at the Alhambra. They hung their coats on the same rack. Easy as pie for Dawson to go to his coat for something — and slip a ten-spot in Zwing's. Betcha a keg of beer he did just that.'

Nor could the others doubt it. Only Durango Joe had had the opportunity to make both plants. 'The rotten skunk!' Curly Max erupted. 'I'll fill his hide so full of lead it'll take ten men to carry his coffin.'

All the rest of them wanted to do the same thing. Joe Dawson had committed the unforgivable sin; he'd double-crossed his own kind. No man in all the border gang had been closer to Curly Max than Zwing Hunter; nor had any of his crew been more loyal to Clem Clayton than Billy Grounds.

The decision to execute Joe Dawson on sight was unanimous. Then another angle of it struck Clem Clayton. Since Joe Dawson had planted the incriminating tens, he must have been one of the two Benson payroll robbers. Thirty-one thousand of the take was safe money. 'And Dawson's got half of it stashed somewhere,' Clem reasoned cannily. 'So we might as well pick it up before we fill him fulla lead.'

It made sense and the others quickly

agreed. 'We'll make him tell who's got the other half,' Curly Max added. 'It's a cinch he's nobody in our bunch. When we know who he is we'll pay him a visit and take it away from him.'

Thirty-one thousand dollars in two quick hauls, plus revenge on Joe Dawson, would certainly beat penny-ante stock steals along the border.

'We'll get an early start in the morning,' Old Man Clayton decided. 'First we make Joe talk. After that I'll match you, Curly, for the first shot at him.'

'The best way to make him talk,' Broccardi advised, 'is to scare hell out of him. The best way to scare hell out of him is to show up with ten or fifteen men and a limber rope. It oughta loosen his tongue, time we choke it a few times under a cottonwood limb. Ike, you and Walt ride into Charleston and pick up a few of Zwing and Billy's best friends. Tell him it's a party and they oughta be in on it.'

\* \* \*

When the party rode out of Charleston at daybreak Friday morning, fourteen gunslung men were in it. Besides Curly Max and the Claytons: there were Dutchy Tyler, Dave Queen, Jerry Barton, Napa Dick, Mort Hicks, Indian Tom, Alex Arnett, Harry Earnshaw, and Lucky Luke Bundy. Any two of them could have handled Joe Dawson. But the lure of thirty-one thousand dollars made everyone want to go, especially those who'd been close to Hunter and Grounds.

And although Dawson himself would be no problem the second of the two Benson robbers was an unknown quantity. He might have a crew around him which would call for an attack in force.

# 19

At his riverbank cabin Joe Dawson slept late Friday morning. There was nothing he could do about Larabee until tomorrow. Tomorrow, Saturday, Larabee would be home from the Vail-Callahan-Larabee roundup. He'd find a cheated partner waiting for him at the L Bar. *I'll make him come clean, or else! I'll build a fire under him and make him give it back!*

But since nothing could be done today, Joe Dawson could only wait and mark time. In mid-morning he got up, dressed, ate breakfast, went out for a look at his pastured horse and then brought a bucket of water from his well. Later he lay on his back, hating Ward Larabee, figuring out just what he'd say to the man. Larabee would of course deny that he'd robbed the snag cache. *But he did it, all right. It couldn't be anyone else.*

Stretched on his back on the cabin cot Joe fed the fires of his fury till early afternoon. Then he dozed an hour and so failed to hear horsemen who drew up outside. His first awareness was when a rough hand shook him awake. 'On your feet, Joe. You got company.'

Durango Joe Dawson sat up, gaping at a roomful of men.

Through an open door he saw others outside. They were men he'd raided with and who'd once been his friends. They looked anything but friendly now. The hand which shook him was Max Broccardi's. To one side stood Clem Clayton and his three gun-weighted sons.

Broccardi yanked Joe from the cot. 'You're taking a ride Joe. Let's go.'

Panic came to Joe Dawson. He looked into the fierce eyes of white-haired Clem Clayton and saw his own death sentence there. 'Whatta yuh want?' he bleated hoarsely. 'I didn't do nothin'.'

'Nothing,' jeered Walt Clayton, 'except frame Zwing and Billy into jail. You planted hot money on 'em, Joe. Somebody fetch his horse and let's ride.'

'You got it all wrong!' Joe protested as

they hustled him outside. 'I didn't . . . '
Harry Earnshaw cut him short with a
hard slap on the mouth.

When he realized that he'd already
been irrevocably condemned by these
men, Joe broke into convulsive sob-
bing. Somehow they knew what he'd
done in a pool game at Tombstone and
in a hotel room at Charleston. Nothing
he could say would make any differ-
ence.

Someone brought his horse, saddled
it, and boosted Joe on it. 'We better get
a mile or so off the trail,' Curly Max decided. He pointed east toward timbered
foothills and they moved that way. Napa
Dick rode ahead and led Joe's horse.
Alex Arnett tossed a lariat over Joe's head
and let the loop lie loosely around his
neck. 'If you want me to jerk it,' Arnett
warned him, 'just try a getaway. You got
a little speech to make, Joe, before we're
through with you.'

They rode into a rincon of the foothills which took them out of sight and
earshot of the Tombstone-Benson stage

road in case a coach or wagon or horseman should come along it. 'What we need for the next half hour,' Broccardi explained, 'is a little privacy.'

A tall lone pine grew in the rincon and Arnett tossed the end of his lariat over a limb. He pulled the rope tight until Joe could feel the loop stinging his neck. Then Dutchy Tyler rode close and tied Joe's hands behind his back. 'I was in that pool game with you and Zwing at the Alhambra. Remember?'

'Make your speech, Joe,' Old Man Clayton commanded. 'And make it quick. Napa, if he don't start speechifyin' in the next minute lead his horse out from under him.'

'You got two choices,' Jerry Barton explained. 'You can talk or dance on air.

Joe's despairing premonition was that he'd dance on air whether he talked or not. These men were mad. He looked at Jerry Barton who was supposed to have killed seventeen men. Killing one more would be as easy, for Jerry Barton, as taking another breath.

'Your minute's half up,' Mort Hicks warned.

'What,' Joe whimpered helplessly, 'do you want me to say?'

Max Broccardi spoke from his left. 'The truth in two packages Joe. Where did you stash your half of the Benson loot?' And who helped you that night?'

'If I tell the truth,' Joe pleaded, 'what happens?'

'We'll turn you loose and give you twenty-four hours to get out of Pima County. But you've got to lead us to your cache, first, and show us the money.'

'I can't,' Joe said desperately. 'He already took it. While I was in Tombstone he crossed me up.'

'You mean the guy who pulled the payroll job with you?' From news accounts it was well known that two men had committed the Benson robbery.

With a rope pinching his throat Joe nodded. 'He's Ward Larabee of the L Bar. He's got my cut and his own hid somewhere on the Cienega. It was him who put me up to it.'

'Put you up to what? Framing Billy Grounds and Zwing Hunter? Alex, tie that rope to the tree. Make it just tight enough so that if we lead his horse out from under him his feet won't quite reach the ground.'

Joe Dawson had nothing more to lose and in desperation he admitted everything. If he could turn their wrath toward Ward Larabee they might even keep their promise and give him twenty-four hours to get out of the county. Which was the most Joe could hope for now.

'Start at the beginning,' Old Man Clayton demanded.

'Joe eased the rope pinch a little by standing in his stirrups. 'His full name's Luther Ward Larabee and he killed a man in Kansas five years ago.' Joe went on to tell about the Lowery brothers helping them raid a corral at Calabasas. A raid which had decoyed a Tucson posse into a chase across the border while Dawson and Larabee were robbing a payroll at Benson. Joe gave them every detail, prompted shrewdly by Curly Max.

At the end Curly Max looked quizzically at Clem Clayton. 'It kinda makes sense, Clem. Whatta yuh think?'

'I got a hunch it's the straight goods, Curly. Always did think there was something phony about that Larabee fella. I happen to know he was thick with Ben Ubrecht. Ben was at my place one time and bragged about knowin' him. The two could've been in together on the Milt O'Hara hold-up.'

'Makes sense to me too,' Earnshaw put in. 'I stopped at the Lowery place last week and I seen an L Bar horse in the pasture there. Asked howcome and they said the owner had to change mounts there one night. Later I rode down the Cienega and saw a Lowery horse grazin' with some L Bar stock. It checks Joe's story about him and Larabee doubling back from Calabasas to Benson and stoppin' to change mounts at the Lowery place.'

'Something else fits too,' Dutchy Tyler added. 'Larabee was in Tombstone about three months ago and I seen him buy a hat in Allen's store there. A hat just like the one that got a hole shot through it at Calabasas.'

Those and other loose threads of fact helped to convince the fourteen outlaws surrounding Joe Dawson. After a few more questions they were ready to accept his charges against Larabee. 'He's got the whole thirty-one thousand dollars salted away somewhere. It's him who put me up to making those plants on Zwing and Billy. So it's him you oughta take it out on, not me.'

Clem Clayton squinted his moist blue eyes. 'Got any ideas where his cache is?'

'I know how you can find it, easy enough,' Joe told them. 'Easy as rollin' off a log. Let me go and I'll tell you.'

Clem was a little to the rear of Joe and Joe failed to see him wink at Curly Max. 'Okay, Joe. Tell us how we can find Larabee's thirty-one thousand dollars and we'll turn you loose.'

Joe hardly believed him. But it was his only chance. Thirty-one thousand dollars made a juicy bait.

'He's got it buried and he keeps a guide sketch in his wallet. I seen him look at it just before he rode at night to bring me a package of the new hot tens.' Joe described the scene accurately, recalling that a round trip to the cache had taken a little more than an hour. 'A mile or so, maybe. He rode upcreek with a spade.'

'Where is he right now?'

'Helping at a mixed roundup in the Empire Hills. But he'll go home in the morning. Nobody at the ranch now but a Mexican woman. You could lay for him and grab that sketch from his wallet.'

Again Broccardi and the elder Clayton exchanged shrewd glances. It would be easy for fourteen armed outaws to intercept Ward Larabee on his way home in the morning. With the sketch to guide them they could go directly to thirty-one thousand buried dollars.

For another while they quizzed Joe Dawson, sifting detail after detail of his story all the way from Calabasas to the finding of a brown paper cigaret snipe by a snag on the San Pedro River. 'It's

297

a fact,' Walt Clayton remembered, 'that the guy smokes brown paper cigarets. I saw him roll one at Tucson.'

'Come to think of it,' Alex Arnett added, I heard Tom Lowery call him Luth one time. The Lowerys came from Kansas and they could've known Larabee there. Me, I'll buy Joe's story all the way. He'd have nothing to gain by ribbin' us.'

'Okay,' Old Man Clayton decided. 'So in the morning we pick up Larabee on his way home from the roundup. After grabbing his cache sketch we'll feed him to the buzzards. Then we dig up the money and hit for Tombstone.' He took out a silver dollar and balanced it in his palm. 'Heads or tails, Curly?'

'What for?'

'We said we'd match for the first shot at him.' Old Man Clayton's grin showed the yellowness of his tobacco-stained teeth. With a nod toward Dawson he drew his forty-five.

'You can't do it,' Joe gasped. 'You promised . . . '

'What we promise a double-crosser don't count. Heads or tails, Curly?'

Broccardi thought a moment and then vetoed the shooting. 'If we shoot him we'll have to bury him. And we forgot to bring along a spade. Let's do it this way.' His spurred boot kicked Joe's horse on the rump and the animal jumped out from under its rider, leaving Joe hanging there. Joe kicked frantically but his feet couldn't quite reach the ground.

The tautness of the noose choked off his screams. 'When they find him' Curly Max assured the others, 'they'll lay it onto some ranch crew who don't like horse thieves. Joe's made a living stealing stock the last season or two. Put a sign on him, Harry.'

Harry Earnshaw found a sheet of paper in his saddlebag and scribbled three words in big letters: HORSE THIEVES, BEWARE.

They pinned it on the dangling Joe Dawson.

Then the avengers from Tombstone and Charleston rode silently back to the river. After splashing across it they took a bee line for the L Bar on Cienega Creek.

'We won't need to talk with him,' Old Man Clayton said. 'Just shoot him on sight and take that sketch from his wallet.'

They rode grimly on, fourteen of the shameless ones. If Zwing Hunter and Billy Grounds, plus five men who'd tried to rescue Gil Stilwell at a water tank, had been with them, it would have been the same band of renegades who'd massacred a peaceful Mexican trading party, not so long ago, near Fronteras below the border.

# 20

This was Altagracia's first train ride. Never before in her seventeen-year-old life had she been on anything faster than a galloping horse. Neither had her roommate, Judy Callahan, now sitting beside her in the coach of a Southern Pacific train chugging eastward toward Pantano station.

When Judy had last taken Altagracia home with her for a week end, in April of the preceding school year, the track had been completed only as far east as Tucson.

Mike Callahan, seated facing them, assured them that his rig would be waiting at Pantano. 'Only an hour from there upcreek to the Circle C and Huachuco'll have supper ready. Beats a five-hour buckboard ride from town all hollow.'

They'd gone straight from Miss Silva's last Friday afternoon class to the depot where they'd boarded this train. It was only an eighteen-mile ride to Pantano.

'The crew's out on roundup,' Callahan told them. 'Won't be anyone there except us and Huachuco.' He pointed south from the coach window to high brown lumps of terrain which people called the Empire Mountains. It's a three-outfit gather: ours and Louee Vail's and Ward Larabee's.'

Mention of Larabee's name brought a shadow to the delicate, sensitive face of Altagracia Casteñada. Her dark eyes had a troubled look as she remembered a face. It was a face she'd seen twice, each time from an upper window. She knew now that the man's name was Ward Larabee and that his ranch was only three miles down the Cienega from Mike Callahan's.

Exactly three weeks ago this Friday evening he'd called in a carriage for Judy. Five nights before that, if Altagracia could believe her eyes, he'd killed Pancho Morales at Calabasas. She'd confided in no one but her cousin Arturo. He'd assured her it was a silly mistake. Later he'd quietly investigated and learned that Larabee had a solid alibi in the person of an honest, old prospector named Packsaddle Jones. 'Señor Larabee is a fine gentleman, Gracia, and we must not insult him with a false charge. It is a sad mistake and you must not speak of it to anyone else.'

She hadn't — not even to Judy.

Yet the matter still preyed on her. She looked out on a mesquite-pocked plain which reached south toward a range of grassy hills where the man Larabee, even now, was helping to round up cattle. She hoped he'd stay there over the week end. Yet she had a feeling he wouldn't. He'd know by now that Judy would be home for Saturday and Sunday. And since he was courting her, Ward Larabee was fairly certain to drop in at the Circle C on one or both of those days. Altagracia could at least be thankful that she hadn't accused him to anyone but Arturo.

A brakeman looked into the coach and shouted 'Pantano.' Presently the train drew up at a new frame depot with a hitchrail back of it. A Circle C team and buckboard had just been tied there by the Pantano liveryman. 'Here we are, girls.' Mike Callahan picked up their satchels and led the way out of the coach.

Shortly they were driving upcreek and midway to the Circle C they passed the L Bar. No one was there but a Mexican woman. 'When do you look for your boss, Maria? Callahan asked her.

'*Manana, señor. Maiiana por la manana.*'

★　★　★

At that same moment two young men were eating supper at the Palace Hotel in Tucson. 'Now look, Roger,' Lynn O'Hara cautioned solemnly. 'We drop by the Callahan place tomorrow and we look plenty surprised when we see the gal there.'

'You can trust me,' Roger Niles promised with a grin. 'I'll say, 'Imagine running into you ladies here!'' His newspaper was giving him the week end off.

'If they ask what we're doing out that

way' Lynn coached him, 'I'll tell 'em I'm looking the Cienega valley over for a land buy. I might want to settle down around here instead of going back to Wyoming.'

'And you talked me into going with you. How early do we start?'

'At daybreak. It's a five-hour saddle ride. So we show up right after they've finished a late breakfast.'

'Arizona ranchers,' Roger confided with a wink, 'are long on hospitality. When a tired traveller drops in they always bring out the *refrescos* and make him rest up for a while. 'Our house is yours,' they always say.'

'It's the best chance you'll ever get, Roger, to be with Altagracia without a *duenna* ridin' hard on you.'

'Where do *you* stand, Lynn? Does Judy know you're coming?'

'If she does she won't admit it.' Lynn finished his coffee and stood up. 'Now we'd better get some sleep, Rog. I've ordered the horses for five o'clock.'

★　★　★

Saturday morning broke warm and cloudless. At a round up camp in the Empire Hills Ward Larabee ate a leisurely breakfast. The crews had already scattered to comb the ravines when Larabee roped and saddled his own mount.

'I'll join you again Monday,' he promised the cook.

In a few minutes he was riding toward his ranch on the Cienega, some eight miles to the northeast. The rising sun was in his eyes and his thoughts were mellow. He'd go home, take a bath and spruce up a little; and then ride upcreek to the Circle C. He knew Judy would be home for the week end. She'd bring her little Spanish roommate and the two would want to go riding. 'They'll need a wrangler, Bucko,' Larabee confided to his buckskin mount. 'So we'll volunteer for the job.'

He decided that the smart time to get there would be just before noon. Huachuco was the best cook on the range and the Circle C was famous for its thick steaks and chokecherry wine. After the midday meal Mike Callahan could be counted on to take his usual siesta and Ward Larabee could go riding with the girls.

There was no hurry. Larabee took his time and presently veered due east toward the far distant tree line of Cienega Creek.

It was half past nine in the morning when he heard a bullet whizz by his head. To his left he saw gunsmoke drift from the rim of an arroyo. Then a fusilade of rifle fire came spitting from three directions — from the left, right, and directly in front. More bullets whistled by and one of them bit at the lobe of Larabee's ear.

Luckily he was riding through six-foot mesquite and by leaning low over the pommel he was able to obscure his head and body from distant sight. Ambushing gunmen were trying to shoot him out of the saddle and he didn't at once try to identify them. Most of the firing came from in front of him and from the north;

so he reined south, hoping to flank and outride any enemies in that direction.

He spurred at breakneck speed through the mesquite and almost ran down a man who was crouched back of a bush with a rifle in hand. The sudden surprise of Larabee's charge at him threw the man off balance and made him miss. A hoof grazed his chest as the hard-running buckskin went by.

And Larabee in a fleeting glance recognized the white hair and beard and fierce, glaring eyes of Old Man Clayton. He heard the man's bellowed curse. Instantly Larabee guessed why he was there; and why a dozen or more border outlaws had come with him. *They're onto me! They're out to get me!*

Rifles were spouting bullets from the north and east. The only direction Larabee could go was south. He leaned low over the buckskin's mane and rode hard, wherever possible keeping under cover of mesquite. The horse squealed when a bullet nipped its flank. Larabee raked it with spurs and when they came to a ditch the horse jumped it, stumbling to fore-knees on the other side. For a despairing breath Larabee thought it was the end. Bullets were snapping through the mesquite and singing only inches overhead. He heard shouting to the left and behind him. 'There he is! Get the son-of-a—' Then the buckskin was up and off again, no bone broken. The animal's panic, no less than Larabee's, lent wings of speed and Larabee reined a little toward the creek line. If he could strike the creek just above his corrals he might turn down it under a screen of brush to his house. But looking sideways to the left he soon saw that he was cut off from that course. They were making sure he couldn't reach his house. Half a dozen riders flanked him in that quarter and as many more came pounding directly behind. He looked back and glimpsed the broad red face of Max Broccardi. These were the border raiders who called themselves 'cowboys' and who for more than a year had terrorized ranches and stagecoaches and Mexican pack trains throughout southeastern Arizona. They were the friends of Zwing Hunter and Billy Grounds. *Joe Dawson, damn him, must have told them what happened. They know I've got the money, all of it, and they're out to get it.*

Too many were on his left and Larabee knew he was hopelessly cut off from the L Bar. His only possible escape was upcreek toward the Circle C.

And the Circle C would make a far safer refuge. His own little ranch house was frame and even if he got to it he'd have to defend it alone. But the Circle C house had thick adobe walls. It had been built as a bastion against Indians; more than once Mike Callahan and his crew had stood off Apache raiders there. Callahan would be there right now and with him there'd be Huachuco and possibly a roustabout or two.

If he could beat his pursuers to Mike Callahan's stout adobe stronghold Larabee felt sure he'd be safe even from the Broccardi-Clayton gang. They were conscienceless outlaws but they'd hardly dare to invade the Callahan premises. Callahan was a power in Arizona with friends at the Tucson courthouse and even in the territorial capital at Prescott. They could hardly break in to kill one of Callahan's guests without killing Callahan himself. And that far, Larabee felt certain, they wouldn't go.

He raced on, bending flat over his pommel. His mount was a thoroughbred and the men chasing him weren't likely to have any horse as swift. He was widening the gap a little. So he veered a bit to the east, angling to strike the creek obliquely. A rider in that direction whipped rifle to cheek and pumped three shots at him. One of them cut a bloody ridge across the back of Larabee's neck. He glimpsed the man and saw that he was Dutchy Tyler of Tombstone, close friend of Zwing Hunter and Max Broccardi.

Tyler fired again and Larabee escaped him by plunging his mount into an arroyo. He rode swiftly down the wash which he knew would take him to the creek not far from his money cache. But as he rounded a bend of the arroyo he came face-to-face with a horseman blocking his path. The man snapped up his rifle and Larabee, with a six-gun in hand, beat him to the trigger pull. He fired point blank and saw the man sway from his saddle. He was Roy Clayton, youngest of the Clayton boys. As Roy fell to the bed of the wash Larabee plunged his mount over him and swept around another bend.

There his horse stepped into a badger hole and stumbled. Immediately it was up and on again. But soon its pace slowed and the animal began favoring its left foreleg, limping slightly. The stumble must have bruised or sprained the leg. It was still more than a mile upcreek to the Callahan place. Could the horse last that long?

The wash opened into the bed of Cienega Creek and here there was occasional willow, cottonwood, and chokecherry cover. Larabee crossed the creek and rode desperately up its east bank, where the cover was thickest. All the pursuers were behind him now. Wherever the cover thinned out, bullets flew at him. Larabee felt blood at his neck and ear and shoulder and knew he'd been scratched at least three times. Only a miracle of luck had saved him from being shot out of the saddle.

Old Man Clayton's screaming voice came from far back of him. 'Get him, Walt! He killed Roy! Cut him off. Fill his dirty hide fulla lead!'

Curly Max Broccardi, riding stirrup to stirrup with him, let out a bellow of his own. 'He's makin' for the Callahan place, boys. Burn him down! Get ahead of him, Ike.'

Could he beat them to Callahan's? Larabee wondered. His bruised mount might fall at any stride. But the only chance was to spur him on. It was less than a mile now to Callahan's with brush cover most of the way. The bullets kept coming. Behind him hooves drummed the creek bottom sand. Riding low Ward Larabee made no attempt to fire back. He must beat them to the Circle C barnyard, jump to the ground there and make a dash for the door. Angry bullets would race him every step of the way.

★ ★ ★

The angriest of the bullets came from Old Man Clayton. Of all the pursuers Clem Clayton had the strongest horse and was now leading the pack. A length or two back of him came Harry Earnshaw, Dutchy Tyler, and Max Broccardi. Walt Clayton, best shot in the gang, had left the creek bed and was loping through a stand of saguaro cacti to the right; that way he could avoid the twists of the creek and perhaps cut Larabee off from the Circle C.

'Get him, Walt!' his father shrieked again.

Clem Clayton's reasons for dealing death to Larabee were now doubled. At the outset there'd been two: revenge for sending Joe Dawson on a sneak mission to plant guilt on Zwing Hunter and Billy Grounds; and to lay hands on a treasure map in Larabee's wallet. Now there were two more reasons: Larabee's horse had run over Clem and left a hoof bruise on his chest; and Larabee's bullet had found the heart of Clem's youngest boy, Roy.

Riding like a maniac, Clem pumped a fresh shell into the chamber of his carbine. His eyes were bloodshot with fury as he whipped the weapon level and fired again.

He could see that Larabee's horse was limping a little. The Circle C buildings were in sight now but the man ahead might not get that far. Not a human was in sight there. A few loose horses were in the corral and an empty buckboard stood in front of the barn. The sprawling adobe house with a parapet around its roof stood like a solid fortress on an eminence facing the creek. Riding to it Larabee would have to cross a stretch of open barnyard and be completely exposed.

As Ward Larabee entered the last stretch of the race he spurred his mount to a run which took him to within twenty yards of the house door. There the bruised animal went down, squealing in pain. It didn't get up. The pursuers saw Larabee land on his feet and race toward the door. 'Get him, Walt!' Clem Clayton shrieked again.

But it was Clem himself who got Larabee. Closer than anyone else he let loose a final volley and two of his slugs caught Larabee full in the back. A dozen other hard-riding outlaws, closing in swiftly, saw Larabee fall face down just outside the ranch house door.

They supposed no one would be inside except Mike Callahan and an Indian cook. According to Joe Dawson the entire Circle C crew was away on fall roundup. Only Callahan and a servant, they supposed, had witnessed the killing of Ward Larabee. Then the door opened and a tall young man sprang out. They saw him take Larabee, dead or dying, by the shoulders and drag him inside. The door slammed.

From within the house came the shocked cry of a girl. The face of a second young man, this one with a bush of yellow hair, showed briefly at a window.

Thirteen outlaws drew rein about seventy yards from the house. Thirteen rifles, hot from shooting at Larabee, were held ready to shoot again. 'We got him!' Clem Clayton said to Max Broccardi.

'We got him all right,' Curly Max admitted sourly. 'But we didn't get what's in his wallet. And Mike Callahan ain't the only one who saw us do it.'

# 21

Watching through a loophole, Lynn O'Hara saw them withdraw a short way to a screen of creek brush. He had no idea why they'd chased Ward Larabee and shot him down at the door of this house. Nor would Larabee himself ever tell. The L Bar man had lived barely a minute after being dragged inside.

A nudge at his elbow made Lynn turn around and see Mike Callahan holding out a repeating rifle. 'Take it and use it, O'Hara. I'm giving you the front of the house.

'You mean you figure they'll come at us? But why? They were after Larabee and they got him. What more would they want?'

Callahan shrugged and made no answer. Instead he went into his gun room and took three more rifles from a rack there. For years he'd kept a ready arsenal for defense against Apaches and outlaws. He came out of the gun room and handed a weapon to his servant Huachuco. 'Take the back side, Huachuco, and watch from the roof. I'll take the south side and defend it from a kitchen window.' He turned to a young yellow-haired reporter from the Tucson *Citizen*. 'Ever shoot a gun, boy?'

Roger Niles took the rifle gingerly. 'At rabbit and quail. Nothing else. You mean ...?'

'I mean get on the roof with that gun. Cover the north side. If they come at us, make a noise with it even if you don't hit anything.'

Rifle in hand, Roger Niles followed Huachuco to the roof. Then two girls came in from the kitchen. The small spanish face of the younger girl had stark terror on it. The one with red hair was of sterner stuff. She'd grown up in this house and more than once she'd seen her father stand off raiders.

He spoke to her quietly. 'Judy, there's a case of ammunition in the gun room closet. Break it open and see that the riflemen are suppied.' To Judy's guest he said gently: I'm sorry for this Gracie. I shouldn't have let Judy bring you here. Looks like we're in for some trouble. You will please go to your room and lie on the floor there, keeping well below the window level.'

'Come with me, Gracie.' Judy Callahan put an arm around the younger girl and they went out together. It left only Lynn and his host in the main *sala*.

Lynn pumped a shell into the chamber of his rifle. It was an army Springfield and he was used to a Winchester 44-40. Arriving here about an hour ago with Roger Niles, he'd unsaddled at the barn and left his own scabbard weapon on the saddle. 'What makes you think they'll come at us?' he asked again.

'Maybe they won't,' the Circle C man said. 'And again maybe they will. We're six witnesses who saw them commit a murder. Always before they've trumped up fake alibis to cheat the hangman. But they can't do it this time. They're goners if they ever let us get to court.'

'It's the Clayton crowd,' Lynn said. 'The whole pack of them. I worked there three weeks and I know 'em.'

'And *I* know them. They know I know them. I know them for cold-blooded killers who'd as lief rub out six witnesses as one. *Sin verguenzas*, my friend Vicente Casteñada calls them. Take a look and see what they're doing now.' Lynn peered through his loophole and for a minute or two fixed a steady gaze on the brush line. 'Two men,' he reported, 'are riding downcreek in the direction they came from. The others are scattering to circle the house. Couple of 'em slipped into the barn and three went to the bunkhouse. Looks like a siege, Mr. Callahan.'

'Call me Mike.' The stockman took a look for himself. 'You're right. I see Curly Max Broccardi peeking out of the bunkhouse. That old white-haired devil Clem Clayton's right with him. I can see Ike Clayton and a gambler named Bundy lookin' us over from the barn. It's the Broccardi-Clayton gangs all in one package.'

'They haven't tossed any slugs yet.'

'Give 'em time. Likely they'll try something else first. Some trick. We'll hold our fire, O'Hara, till they open up on us.'

'Wonder what they sent those two men down the creek for.'

Callahan didn't answer until he'd made the rounds of the house. Ten quiet minutes slipped by. Lynn looked at the mantel clock and was surprised to see that it was only eleven in the morning. Then he looked down at a stain on a rug where Ward Larabee had breathed his last breath. Huachuco had quickly removed the body to his own quarters off the kitchen and covered it with a blanket.

Mike Callahan rejoined Lynn with a speculation on Lynn's last question. 'Could be they dropped something while they were chasing Larabee; and sent two men back for it Or maybe one of 'em got hit and needs to be picked up. It still leaves about a dozen of 'em squattin' around us like wolves. Back of the house, two men are aiming rifles at us over a corral wall. Dutchy Tyler and a killer named Mort Hicks. Three more of 'em are to the north of us lying flat in a dry irrigation ditch. Napa Dick, Indian Tom and Jerry Barton.'

Lynn weighed the possibilities. 'If I were in their place, I'd high-tail deep into Mexico and stay there.'

'Trouble is,' Callahan countered, 'that some of them are property owners here in Arizona. The Claytons, for instance, would lose a pretty good little cattle and hay ranch on the San Pedro. Curly Max owns a saloon at Galeyville and Harry Earnshaw's got one at Harshaw. Most of 'em have filed on land and built a cabin on it. They've got these little ranches stocked with calves born of stolen Mexico cows. If they leave Arizona for keeps, they lose all that.'

'So the only way they can stay in Arizona,' Lynn summed up, 'is to make sure not one of us leaves this house alive.'

Callahan brooded silently for a minute, then began thinking aloud. 'They can't quite be sure how many of us are in here. Maybe that's why they haven't opened up. We won't fire till they do. Then all five of us will answer, each with one shot from a different loophole. It'll make 'em think we've got at least five guns and are defending all sides of the house.'

'Five?' Lynn questioned. 'We're only four.'

Judy'll make five,' her father said grimly. 'I'll tell her to shoot once when we do and then duck low. No use askin' Gracie to do that. She wouldn't be up to it.'

Callahan went out to make the rounds again and to give instructions. Lynn kept watch at his front loophole, from which he could see the creek brush, the barn, and half the bunkhouse. Beyond the creek he saw tethered horses, still saddled. No human was in sight. But a cigaret snipe, thumped away by a human hand, came sailing out of the bunkhouse door.

What, he puzzled, had made them

chase and kill Ward Larabee? And could they be sure they'd killed him? They'd seen him shot down and dragged inside but he might still be alive.

Judy Callahan, wearing moccasins, came quietly into the *sala* with a heavy rifle in her hands. She took a stand at a loophole about three steps from Lynn's. 'Father told me what to do,' she said.

Lynn looked at her and nodded. 'We don't shoot till they do. Then we let them hear five bangs from five spots. Maybe if we're lucky we'll even hit one of 'em.'

'Gracie would make six,' Judy murmured. 'But she can't of course. She's the timid sort. It would scare her to death even to touch a loaded rifle.'

'I'm not so sure of that,' Lynn said. 'She's scared but shes not panicky. Arturo told me she was raised on a ranch down at Magdalena. They've got Apaches and outlaws down there too.'

Mike Callahan's voice shouted from a kitchen window where he was guarding the south side of the house. 'They're about to open up, I think. Rifles are pointing at us from all directions. Get ready to return fire. But only one shot from each gun.'

He was echoed by a fusilade of rifle fire which came from all quarters of the compass. From the creek line, the barn, the bunkhouse, the corral, the irrigation ditch. Bullets thudded into the house's adobe walls and splintered a window shutter. One of the slugs crashed through the oak of the front door, zinged across the *sala* and chipped plaster from an inner wall.

Lynn promptly poked his rifle barrel through his loophole and fired at the open bunkhouse door. Judy did the same at another loophole, firing at a puff of smoke hanging against the creek brush. A shot cracked from Mike Callahan's rifle in the kitchen. Then Lynn distinctly heard three shots fired from the roof.

'Huachuco must have fired twice,' Judy said.

'Either him or Roger Niles,' Lynn agreed.

The next ten minutes brought no

sound except a ticking from the mantel clock. Peering out Lynn failed to see any sign of the besiegers. They were probably taking stock now that they knew the house had defenders on all four sides.

Behind him Lynn heard Mike Callahan skip up steps to the roof. He'd be making the rounds to be sure that none of his force had been hit.

When he came down his face wore an odd look. 'What do you know?' he murmured incredulously.

'All I know,' Lynn said, 'is that Huachuco or Niles cut loose twice. You told 'em to shoot only once.'

'Each of them *did* shoot only once,' Callahan announced with a bewildered shake of his head. 'Believe it or not the other shot was fired by our timid little guest Altagracia. She found a .38 rabbit gun and went up to the roof with it. Right now she's kneeling behind a parapet there alongside of Roger Niles.'

Judy couldn't believe it. 'Not Gracie!' she exclaimed in open-mouthed wonder. She looked at Lynn and gave a half hysterical laugh. 'What would Miss Silva think of us now?'

'I know what *I* think of you.' Lynn looked at Judy's flushed face and added, 'Remind me to tell you some time.'

Mike Callahan grimaced and gave a shrug. 'You never can tell what a woman'll do when the chips are down. The way it stands now, those hyenas out there think we've got six real guns waitin' for 'em. If they charge us in daylight, they'll have to figure on losing six men before they crash in on us. So they might wait till nightfall.'

The mantel clock struck eleven-thirty. Nightfall would come in less than eight hours.

Callahan went back to his post and Lynn, with Judy only a few steps away, kept his watch at the front. 'Is there any chance of the roundup crew coming back?'

'Not today,' Judy reasoned. 'There's a bare chance of it tomorrow, Sunday. One of them might ride back here on Sunday to replace a piece of equipment. Or the cook might want another sack of flour.'

But Lynn had a feeling the issue would be decided before tomorrow. In daylight they could perhaps stand off the besiegers but in the dark the outlaws could creep up unseen from four sides. Shuttered windows could be smashed in simultaneously and the house invaded like pirates boarding a ship at sea.

'They're coming back,' Judy announced from her loophole. 'The two men who rode down the creek. They're leading a horse.'

Lynn looked and saw that the led horse had a blanket-wrapped body draped over it. Apparently it was a casulty in the gunfire chase after Larabee. The two outlaws leading the dead man's horse passed out of sight behind the bunkhouse.

'There was a fired shell in Larabee's six-gun,' Lynn remembered. 'Looks like he fired back at them and got his man.'

Another interval of quiet was followed by a surprise. Old Man Clayton walked boldly out of the bunkhouse with a white flag in his hand. It looked like a pillow slip strung on the end of a hoe handle. Waving it Clem Clayton came directly toward the ranch house.

'He wants a truce,' Lynn shouted to Mike Callahan. 'Wants to parley about something.'

Callahan came quickly from the kitchen. As he passed the roof stairs he shouted up, 'Watch out for a trick.'

Clem Clayton, waving his flag, came on to the house and knocked. 'Whatever he says,' Lynn whispered to Judy, 'don't believe him. He's as full of lies as a dog has fleas.'

Mike Callahan opened a small circular port in the door and glared out through it. 'That's far enough, Clayton. Speak your piece from there.'

Clayton gave it glibly. 'Ward Larabee killed my boy Roy in cold blood. We tried to make a citizen's arrest so we could turn him over to the sheriff. But he took off this way. All we did was stop him with a bullet. How's he doin'?'

'He's dead,' Callahan said coldly. 'So you might as well leave us alone and go home.'

The watery blue eyes of Clem Clayton took a scheming squint. It was clear that one of his reasons for coming to the house had been to make certain that Larabee was dead. Since he was dead, the L Bar man couldn't have revealed he'd had to run a race with bullets.

'When Larabee killed my boy Roy,' Clem explained craftily, 'he stole a sketch map out of Roy's pocket. It's a guide Roy made to an outcrop of silver ore he found and the map show how to go to it. Larabee killed him for it and put it in his wallet. Just then the rest of us rode up and he high-tailed this way. Give us that guide map and we'll ride away and leave you alone.'

'Wait a minute,' Callahan said, 'while I take a look. Keep an eye on him, O'Hara. Judy, run up to the roof and tell Hank and Alfredo to open up if they start shooting again.'

Judy nodded and went promptly to the roof. Her father, of course, was trying to make Clayton think that three of the regular ranch crew were helping defend the house.

As Mike Callahan withdrew to the rear, Clayton's voice came slyly from outside. 'He ain't foolin' me none. I know who's here and who ain't.'

Lynn ignored him. And presently Callahan came back from Huachuco's sleeping quarters where he'd inspected the wallet in the dead man's pocket.

'There *is* a guide sketch,' he admitted to Clem Clayton 'in Larabee's wallet. But it's one he made himself. It's on a letter-head of the L Bar ranch. The terrain it describes is one I know very well. And it's a long way from any silver outcrop. Looks to me like Larabee buried something there and made sure he could go back to it. He must have had an honest reason because Ward Larabee was no stagecoach robber like you and those hellion boys of yours, Clayton.'

The insult to his sons angered Old Man Clayton and he bellowed out things he hadn't intended to mention. 'The hell he wasn't! He was a crook and a killer from away back. Killed a man in Kansas before he ever came here. Helped Ben Ubrecht rob and kill Milton O'Hara. He killed a Mexican peon at Calabasas a few weeks back while he was raidin' a corral; then doubled back north to stick up a payroll at Benson. Put up against the likes of Larabee, my boy Roy was lily white.'

It came spitting out venomously from the lips of a man choked with frustration and fury. While he was speaking Judy returned from the roof and rejoined them. With her father and Lynn she stood shocked and completely incredulous. One small charge against a reputable neighbor like Ward Larabee they might have believed, but not a whole string of charges all spelling murder. Lynn saw a stunned look on Judy's face as though she herself had been dealt a personal blow. Clayton was talking about a man who'd taken her to a ball only three weeks ago last night; a man who was frankly hoping to marry her and who had the tacit approval of her father.

'You can't fool us with a pack of lies,' Callahan retorted through the door. 'Now if that's all you've got to say, get back under cover before we start bouncing bullets off you.'

'We're thirteen to four,' Clayton warned him, 'or maybe five. And we aim to have that sketch map. We'll give you till dark to hand it over.'

'And if we don't?'

'If you don't we wipe you out. All of you. Easy enough after it's dark. Only chance you've got's to hand over that map.'

Mike Callahan, standing back of his oaken door, gave it a judicious consideration. Then he called out his decision. 'If I thought you'd really ride away and leave us alone, I'd give it to you. But I know you, Clem Clayton. Whether or not we give you the map, you'd wipe us out just as quick as you wiped out those Mexican traders at Fronteras. You're entirely without conscience or shame. We saw you kill Larabee and you don't dare let us tell about it in court.'

'What I said stands,' Clayton warned

again. 'You've got till nightfall. If you don't hand it over by then, people'll think a band of Apaches've been raiding here.' He turned and walked angrily back to the bunkhouse.

In the *sala* Lynn was still looking at the shocked face of Judy Callahan. In a moment she exclaimed, 'imagine him saying those horrible things about Ward Larabee!'

Her father slipped an arm around her. 'Forget it, Judy. It was just a pack of lies . . . '

'But it wasn't, Señor Callahan.' The small voice of Altagracia Casteñada spoke from the roof stairs. 'I have heard what he said. And some of it is the truth.'

As they stared at her, Judy was the first to find voice. 'You can't mean that, Gracie! He even said that Mr. Larabee killed that *vaquero* of yours at Calabasas.'

'Which is true,' the little Spanish girl told them sadly. 'I, from my window, saw it with my own eyes. This I have told to my cousin Arturo but he does not believe.'

# 22

The mantel clock struck noon as the girl from Magdalena made her sensational and preposterously unbelievable charge against Ward Larabee. For a moment it left both Judy and her father speechless.

Then Judy gave a confused protest. 'What are you saying? It can't be . . . '

'Of course it can't,' Mike Callahan cut in. He was sure that the terrors of the siege had somehow twisted the girl's mind into thinking white was black. 'Look, Gracie. You better quit the roof and stay in the kitchen. Judy, go help her make some coffee and sandwiches. We men'll take turns about reporting there for a snack.'

Obediently Judy left her loophole and went to the foot of the roof stairs. Her guest meekly joined her and the two girls disappeared into the kitchen.

It left the roof guarded only by Huachuco and Roger Niles. 'They can't look four ways at once,' Callahan said gruffly to Lynn. 'Let's go up there and help 'em.'

Lynn followed him to the roof. Its parapets were thirty inches high and by crawling to positions on all fours they kept out of sight from besiegers. Callahan took the south side and Lynn took the east. Huachuco and Niles were kneeling back of the other two parapets. 'See anything of them Rog?' Lynn asked.

'I see three men in a ditch, whenever they raise up a little.'

'Did you hear what Old Man Clayton said about Larabee?'

'Yes. He called Larabee a thief and a killer.'

'Do you believe it?'

'No. Do you?'

'Yes.' Lynn's blunt affirmative came as a jolt to both Roger Niles and Mike Callahan. He went on to sum up quickly. 'I talked with Arturo Casteñada and he said Gracie made the same charge to him. Arturo checked with Larabee who alibis himself with an old prospector named Packsaddle Jones. But the alibi won't be solid till we check again with the San Xavier priests. Arturo promised to do that the first chance he gets. Meantime we find border thieves chasing Larabee with bullets. Why? Because he's got a sketch map and they want it. They claim he robbed a payroll at Benson. If he did he'd need to bury the loot and make sure he could find it again. And when we look in his wallet we find just what Clem Clayton claims is there. Then Gracie backs it all up.'

Before anyone could argue with him a volley of shots came from the bunkhouse and another from behind a corral wall at the rear. Bullets thumped into the parapets and sang overhead. One of them came through a loophole and flicked dust in Lynn's eyes. Only Huachuco fired back and his shot brought a yell from the corral. It was followed by a profane exclamation from one of the outlaws there. 'They got Dutchy, Mort! He's hit bad!'

'Good shooting, Huachuco,' Callahan

applauded. 'It shaves the odds a little. After this, whenever we get a fair bead on one of 'em, we take it . . . I still can't believe what Gracie says about Larabee.'

Lynn countered, 'If it turns out he lied about his alibi we'll *have* to believe her.'

'How can we know whether he lied or not?'

'By a priest at San Xavier. He'll tell us the day Packsaddle Jones attended a mass there.'

For a while there was no more shooting. Then Judy called from the stair well. 'Lunch is ready in the kitchen. Come one at a time.'

'You go first, Niles,' Callahan ordered. 'While you're eating keep a watch out the south kitchen loophole. It looks to a feed lot. Three men are behind the mud wall and one of them's Walt Clayton.'

Rifle in hand, Roger slithered back to the stair well and disappeared down it.

A moment later he joined two girls in the kitchen. Altagracia handed him a cold beef sandwich and a cup of coffee. Her delicate face was tear-stained. 'They do not believe me, Roger.'

He didn't even marvel that she'd call him Roger. One hour together behind a parapet with bullets thumping it was like a lifetime. Roger Niles took his handkerchief and wiped away her tears. '*I* believe you, Gracie.'

'You do?' she exclaimed gratefully.

'Sure. I'm a news reporter and I don't believe in coincidences. It would be too much of a coincidence if you and Old Man Clayton came to the same wrong conclusion about Larabee.'

Judy, warming up yesterday's tortil at at the stove, made no comment. A mixture of confusion and mortification seemed to hold her in a spell.

'I am sorry that I told only Arturo,' Gracie said bleakly. 'If I had told also the sheriff, perhaps Señor Larabee would be in jail instead of leading the shameless ones to this house. Now they wish to kill us. They are thirteen and our men are only four.'

'They're only twelve,' Roger corrected. 'Huachuco got one of them.' He looked through a kitchen loophole at the adobe wall of a feed lot. Three men were peering over it and one of them, Walt Clayton, was aiming his rifle this way. *If I was any good at shooting, Roger thought, I'd try to pick him off. But I'd miss and it would only draw fire to the kitchen.*

Someone on the roof had another idea. A rifle cracked up there and Roger saw one of the feed lot outlaws collapse out of sight. One more of 'em down,' he told the girls. 'Leaves only eleven.'

Horror on Altagracia's face made him shift the subject. 'Tell me about the San Xavier mission, Gracie. Lynn figures on the priests there checking an alibi for us.'

'It is the oldest and most famous mission on the *camino real*,' she told him. 'The good Father Kino founded it more than a hundred years ago. We of Mexico call it *La Paloma Blanca del Desierto*.'

'The White Dove of the Desert!' Roger repeated. 'What days do they hold mass there?'

'On all days of the week,' Gracie said. 'Or on any day that a weary traveller comes by for rest and comfort, and requests one.'

'If Packsaddle Jones was there on a Wednesday he couldn't have gotten to the L Bar before Thursday. Which'd shoot Larabee's alibi sky high.'

Roger finished his sandwich and Judy said, 'I'll call one of the others now.'

She went up to the roof but came back alone. 'Father wants you to stay here with Gracie,' she told Roger Niles. 'Don't let her go near a window or door. I'll take lunch up to them.' She filled a tray and went to the roof with it.

When she came down Lynn O'Hara was with her but they didn't come into the kitchen. Instead they took their old posts at loopholes in the main *sala* which looked out on the bunkhouse and barn. It left Huachuco and Mike Callahan on the roof.

From the kitchen Roger and Gracie heard the mantel clock strike one. Another hour had slipped by in the lives of two young men and two girls facing death together. No rule or convention of the Silva school had any significance now.

An occasional volley of gunfire came from the besiegers. Answering shots could be heard now and then from the roof. In the kitchen Roger Niles held his fire, merely watching to be sure no one advanced from the feed lot. Twice they heard Lynn O'Hara take a shot at the bunkhouse or barn. *They're playing cat-and-mouse*, Roger concluded, *waiting till nightfall*. He didn't mention his thought to Gracie. Instead he said brightly: 'I got a feeling our luck's due to change. I mean I've a hunch help'll show up, somehow.'

'It would take a miracle from the saints,' she murmured.

'This is a good time to believe in miracles. Don't you think?'

She looked at him with a grave nod. 'Always it is a good time to have faith.'

In the main *sala* Lynn O'Hara was saying: 'If we get out of this, Judy, I'm not going back to Wyoming. I like it here in Arizona.'

'But how *can* you like it here?' Judy

wondered. 'Here on a lawless border where they killed your brother?'

'I like it here because you're here, Judy.' Lynn said it with a direct simplicity and it didn't occur to her that he was presumptuous. He'd been in this house only five hours — but in five years she couldn't have known him better.

'Tell me about your brother Milton,' she said presently. 'Was he married?'

'No. I was the only family he had. He was ten years older — took care of me when I was a kid. He always said he'd set me up in the cow business some day.' A shot from the barn splintered through the front door and the bullet missed Judy only by inches. Lynn reached out and pulled her toward him. 'Keep away from that door.' He spoke angrily. 'Sit on the floor with your back to a wall.'

To his surprise she obeyed him. Another shot came and again splinters flew inward from the door. Any one of those devils out there, Lynn thought savagely, could be the man who'd helped Ubrecht rob and kill Milton O'Hara.

Clem Clayton said the other man was Larabee. Maybe. Maybe not. They were all of a breed, the Clayton-Broccardi crew of border outlaws and Ward Larabee.

'If you stay in Arizona,' Judy asked, 'will you file on land?'

'More likely I'll buy a ready-made ranch if I can get a bargain. And I've thought of a likely one. The L Bar. I'd be your Dad's closest neighbor.'

'The L Bar? But it's not for sale.'

'It will be,' Lynn prophesied grimly. 'Larabee can't use it any more.'

A few hours ago she would have been shocked but now she only asked curiously, 'Do you really believe what that awful man said about him?'

'I believe what Gracie says about him. And I believe the cache map he carried in his wallet will show where he buried the Benson payroll money. More than likely he helped Ben Ubrecht rob and kill my brother.'

'Your brother sold a mining claim at Tombstone, didn't he?'

'Yes. And sent most of the money to a bank in Cheyenne. He planned for us to start a cattle spread with it. I can still use that way — and the ranch can be Larabee's. It would be a sort of justice . . . and I think my brother would want it like that. He was on his way to give me a start in the cattle business. Larabee stopped him — but on the L Bar I'd still be getting the start with Larabee's land and brand.'

Before the clock struck three a half dozen more rounds of fire came from the besiegers. Each was answered from the roof. From his own loophole Lynn saw Ike Clayton peering from the barn door and fired at him. It was a miss and drew a jeer from Ike. 'Have fun while you can, O'Hara. Your deadline's nightfall and you're number one on my list, cowboy.'

'His old man must've told him I'm here,' Lynn concluded. 'They've likely got it in for me on account of what happened at the Rillito water tank. Five of their pals had bad luck there.'

When the clock struck four Altagracia was saying to Roger Niles in the kitchen, 'The last time my father and I stopped at the San Xavier mission, on our way up the *camino real*, we lighted a candle to the Mother Mary.'

To Roger it didn't seem at all irrelevant. 'Let's hope that candle's still burning, Gracie. If we ever get out of this we'll go back there and light another. Tell me more about Father Kino.'

She told him more about the most illustrious of the pioneer priests who, more than a century before, had crossed the mountains and deserts of Mexico to establish San Xavier del Bac near which had later sprung up the little plaza of Tucson. 'Father Anselmo is there now,' Gracia said. 'It is he who . . .'

She got no farther because of a sudden and heavy rifle fire which came from all directions. A bullet cut through the window shutter and clanged on the metal of the stove. Roger pushed Gracie to the floor where he held her below the sill level. From bunkhouse, barn, ditch, feed lot, and corral the shots kept coming, round after round. Roger could hear Lynn firing from the front *sala* while other shots sounded from the roof.

He remembered his own responsibility and got to his feet. 'Keep low, Gracie.' From his loophole he saw two men in the feed lot firing this way. *If I could only pick off one of them!* Roger thrust his rifle barrel through the hole, aimed and fired. But he had no skill with guns. It was a wide miss.

Then the firing stopped and he heard someone coming down from the roof. The voice of Mike Callahan spoke somberly to those in the front *sala*. 'You stay downstairs, Judy. O'Hara, you'd better come up to the roof with me. We'll each have to guard two sides of it now.'

'What about Huachuco?' Lynn asked.

'He's dead. That last volley got him. It's up to you and me now, O'Hara.'

From the kitchen Roger heard the mantel clock strike five. In two hours the light would be fading. In three it would be quite dark. Huachuco had been a crack shot and the ablest defender. 'Me, I'm no good,' Roger said miserably to Alta-gracia. She'd moved to a corner and was sitting with her back to the wall. 'You're right about one thing, Gracie. It'd take a miracle from the saints to get us out of this.'

'We must not despair,'she said.

# 23

At that moment the miracle was riding eastward across the mesquite prairie which reached from the Empire Hills to Cienega Creek. It was a party of seven men and its leader was the sheriff of Pima County.

One of the riders spoke impatiently. 'Why don't we go straight to the L Bar and pick him up?'

'Because first,' Sheriff Shibell answered him, 'I want to talk with your little cousin. If she looks me straight in the eye and accuses Larabee, and swears she saw him shoot Morales at Calabasas, that'll be all I need. We'll ride three miles down the creek and pick him up. All we know for sure is that he lied about an alibi.'

They spurred to a fast trot, heading toward the Circle C. The Cienega tree line wasn't yet in sight. With the addition of Arturo Casteñada, this was exactly the same posse which, nearly four weeks ago, had been decoyed into a chase after horse thieves across the border.

'Father Anselmo,' Arturo again assured his chief, 'remembers the date very well. It was Wednesday, September first. On the first day of each month he always puts fresh wicks in the mission lamps. He was doing that when Pack-saddle Jones arrived.'

'So he read a mass for Jones and let him rest there through the noon heat. Packsaddle got away, he said, about two in the afternoon?'

'That is right,' Arturo confirmed. 'Later in Tombstone he told Lynn O'Hara that he camped overnight in the Empire Hills and got as far as the L Bar for lunch the next day. With burros a man cannot travel faster than that.'

'Which puts him at Larabee's place at noon Thursday,' Shibell agreed, 'eighty-four hours after the killing at Calabasas. Which knocks Larabee's alibi into a cocked hat.'

They pressed on silently for another mile, a grim sheriff and six deputies who'd recently lost face by failure to catch up with the Calabasas raiders. Now was a chance to make up for it and bring the killer to justice. But Father Anselmo and Packsaddle Jones were only circumstantial witnesses. The one eye witness was Altagracia Casteñada and Shibell, upon Arturo's return from an Xavier, had gone straight to Miss Silva's school to question the girl. 'She is spending the week end,' Miss Silva had informed him, 'with her roommate at the Circle C.'

And since the Circle C was only three miles out of their way to the L Bar, the posse was heading directly there.

Behind them the sun set back of the Empire Hills and in front of them the Cienega tree line came in sight.

Then distant popping sounds made Shibell draw up alertly. 'Do you hear that, Julio? Sounds like gunfire.' His posse reined up by him.

Undersheriff Julio Caballero wasn't too impressed. He shrugged his plump shoulders and licked a cigaret. 'It is Saturday evening,' he said. 'The crew is perhaps home for the week end. They perhaps amuse themselves by shooting bottles off the corral wall.'

'Maybe,' the sheriff admitted. 'But let's make sure.' He spurred to a lope and his men followed, whipping through the mesquite toward brown adobe walls in the valley ahead.

\* \* \*

Lynn O'Hara and Mike Callahan crouched back of roof parapets and each of them had to watch in two directions. Lynn had posted himself at the roof's northeast corner from which he could cover barn, bunkhouse and ditch; while Callahan at the southwest corner overlooked the corral and feed lot, each of which was fenced with a five-foot adobe wall.

For the past half hour there'd been spasmodic firing from the corral and bunkhouse but the defenders weren't firing back. Exposing a head or an elbow was too risky. 'Just the two of us left,'

Callahan reminded Lynn. The young newsman downstairs didn't really count except as a look out. 'If they get one of us the other wouldn't stand a chance.' He was thinking not of himself but of the two girls below stairs.

Lynn looked up at a cloudy sky. Tonight there'd be no moon or stars. When inky darkness came they wouldn't be able to see eleven attackers creeping up on all sides. 'We've got an hour or two of light left.'

The blond head of Roger Niles showed at the stair well. 'Do you need me up here?' he asked.

'Not yet,' Callahan answered him. 'Just keep the girls away from doors and windows. Then keep circling the house from side to side and watch for signs of attack. When it gets too dark to see anything, bring the girls up here and we'll have them sit in the center of the roof.'

'Shall I light a lamp?'

'No. Keep the house dark.'

Roger disappeared and Lynn, looking toward the barn, saw a man's elbow and half his cheek showing at the doorway. He'd spotted the man before and identified him by his black and white checkered shirt. 'It's Luke Bundy. Shall I take a crack at him?'

'Use your own judgment,' Callahan advised dubiously. Cutting down the besiegers from eleven to ten would help a little, but hardly in proportion to the risk of reducing the house's effective garrison from two to one.

Lynn got to his knees and aimed over the top of the parapet. It exposed his head and drew half a dozen shots from the bunkhouse and barn. The bullets chipped dust from the top of the wall and it stung Lynn's eyes as he squeezed the trigger. A cry of pain from the barn meant that he'd winged Bundy. 'Leaves ten of 'em,' Lynn reported as he ducked under cover.

From the opposite side of the house came a terrific rattle of shooting. It was from the corral and should have sent streams of bullets into the parapet walls. Strangely it didn't. Callahan spoke in a puzzled voice. 'Somethin' funny goin' on out there. They're tossin' lead but not in our direction.'

The answer came in an oncoming drum of hoofbeats. Seven horsemen burst out of the mesquite on the corral side of the house, each rider blazing away with a rifle. Bullets were sweeping the corral and to the right of it caught the irrigation ditch lengthwise in enfilade.

It gave no cover to three outlaws who until now had lain screened behind the crown of the ditch. Looking that way Lynn saw Napa Dick, Indian Tom, and Jerry Barton get up and race for the bunkhouse. Bullets from the posse chased them. Two of them were hit and fell facedown in the ditch. The third man, Barton, kept running and Lynn drew a bead on him. He fired and dropped the man just as he reached the bunkhouse steps.

On his own side of the roof Mike Callahan was tripping his trigger. 'They're on the run!' he shouted; and Lynn knew he meant the feed lot men. 'They're legging it for the creek.' The saddled horses,

Lynn remembered, had been left in the creek brush.

To the west of the corral the posse had stopped, dismounted, and were advancing afoot through the mesquite, shooting it out with the corral outlaws. On his own side Lynn heard men running toward the creek, keeping bunkhouse and barn between them and the house. He glimpsed the burly figure of Max Broccardi racing toward his horse, fired too quickly, and missed him. A bit to the left Old Man Clayton and his son Ike were sprinting toward the brush and Lynn emptied his rifle at them. He saw Clem fall but Ike kept running on.

It was a rout and Mike Callahan gave a jubilant cheer. 'It's all over, boy! The corral men are giving up.'

Lynn joined him and beyond the corral he saw seven men advancing in a crouch. He recognized Sheriff Shibell, Arturo Casteñada, and Julio Caballero. Two outlaws in the corral had dropped their rifles and stood with hands raised. 'How many got away, O'Hara?'

'Only three, I think,' Lynn said. The three were out of range now. He saw them get to their horses and spur swiftly away, heading southeast toward Charleston. 'Curly Max is one of them. Other two look like Ike and Walt Clayton.'

'They'll be rounded up some day,' Callahan predicted. He leaned over the parapet and shouted to the posse. 'Howdy, Sheriff. They've been gunning hell out of us all day. Who the devil tipped you we were in trouble?'

'Nobody,' Shibell shouted back. 'But we got a tip on Larabee. Got it from a mission priest. We were heading for the L Bar to pick him up.'

'You don't have to go any further, Sheriff.'

Lynn didn't wait to hear more. He ran down the steps to the main *sala*. Judy was there with a smudge of gunpowder on her face. For the first time she looked pale and frail and weary to the edge of collapse. Lynn wanted to take her in his arms but lacked the courage for it. All he could do was ask lamely, 'Are you all right, Judy?'

'Never mind me. What about Dad?' She rushed up to the roof to find out.

It left Lynn alone in the front room and from there he went to check on Gracie and Roger in the kitchen. He expected to find the little Spanish girl in a state of collapse.

The sudden release, after the hours of terror she'd been through, could be enough to break down even a robust man.

Instead he found her with bright cheeks and shining eyes, and with her hands clutching Roger's. Her tumbled dark hair made a frame for her as she looked up at him. All the inhibitions of her sheltered life had been swept away. 'We shall go to the mission, Roger, and light the candle.'

'Lots of them,' Roger said earnestly. 'When your school is over I shall ask your father to meet me there with you on his arm. Just the four of us: you, me, your Dad, and a priest. Is it a date, Altagracia?'

It was the first time he'd ever spoken her full name and it sounded beautiful. Her lips said nothing but her excited eyes said yes. As Roger leaned forward to kiss her they didn't know that Lynn O'Hara stood in the doorway, ruefully abusing his own cowardice.

# 24

Dark came within the hour and lamps flooded the Callahan house with light. Weary horses stood hipshot at the corral fence. The girls were resting in a bedroom while Mike Callahan held a parley with Shibell, Casteñada, Caballero, Lynn O'Hara, and Roger Niles.

Shibell glanced at a memo he'd just made. 'I've tallied the losses, Mike. You lost one man on your side. Of the thirteen on the other side, they tally out five dead, two wounded, three unhit prisoners, and three who got away. The escapees are Broccardi and two of the Clayton boys.'

'Maybe they'll run into the Earp brothers some day,' Julio Caballero remarked hopefully, 'down around Tombstone.'

'You can add two more to the dead list,' Callahan said. 'In a running fight this morning Ward Larabee killed Roy Clayton and then got drilled himself.'

Shibell nodded. He'd already taken

a sketch map from the wallet of a dead man who lay under a blanket on Huachuco's cot. 'They must've wanted this pretty bad to shoot up the house for it.'

'The main reason they shot up the house,' Callahan reminded them, 'was to keep us from telling on them in court. You'll see a spring marked on that map, Sheriff, at the edge of the creek about halfway between here and the L Bar. It's right opposite a cedar tree and easy to find. Why don't you send a crew down there with lanterns and a spade? They can pace from landmark to landmark and find the spot marked X.'

'If Old Man Clayton told the truth,' Lynn added, 'you'll find buried money there. Maybe half or all of the Benson payroll.'

Shibell handed the map to his undersheriff. 'Julio, take two men and lanterns and a spade. Find the spot and dig up whatever's there. Bring it right here. And send one man to Pantano station to telegraph the news to Tucson.'

'If you don't mind I'll go along too,'

Roger Niles offered. 'I want to wire my paper so they can put out an extra edition.'

'No way I can stop you,' Shibell said. He turned wearily to Callahan. 'What about some grub and coffee, Mike?'

It was after midnight when Caballero's detail got back. The girls were sleeping the sleep of exhaustion. Eight dead men, including Huachuco, Larabee, and Roy Clayton, lay under sheets in the bunkhouse. Three prisoners, Hicks, Queen, and Arnett, stood manacled in a padlocked saddle room. The wounds of Bundy and Earnshaw had been treated but neither was in any condition to escape. No attempt had been made to chase Broccardi and the two surviving Claytons.

'Here she is, Chief.' Julio Caballero laid a clay-stained metal box on the kitchen table. 'I counted it and it comes to thirty-one thousand dollars.'

Shibell verified the amount and smiled grimly. 'It's every dollar of the Benson money except those two packages of new tens.'

'My guess,' Lynn offered, 'is that the tens were planted on Hunter and Grounds; and it made the Claytons so mad they went gunning for Larabee.'

Roger Niles, who'd returned from Pantano station, made a report of his own. 'I wired my paper and there'll be an extra on the street in the morning.'

The deputy who'd gone to Pantano with Roger added: 'I notified the courthouse and there'll be a coroner here tomorrow. And I got a piece of news myself from Ike Brokow.'

'What's new with Brokow?' Shibell asked.

'He just added three more to the population of his jail. Couple of barroom bruisers and a gambler named Shonsey. Seems the bruisers got drunk and bragged about how Shonsey had paid 'em a hundred dollars for beating up Lynn O'Hara.' The deputy looked at Lynn with a grin. 'So you were wrong, cowboy, when you figured it was border outlaws who jumped you.'

Mike Callahan refilled the coffee cups all around and then Roger Niles beckoned Lynn aside for a private word. 'I sent another wire,' he reported, 'to Miss Silva at the school. Told her the girls are okay and not to worry. Told her they'd be taken back to town soon as they get good and rested.'

All through Sunday and Monday the Circle C swarmed with lawmen, a mortician's crew, a coroner, reporters from both the Tucson weeklies, and curious neighbors. Along with them came Cashier Hudson of the Safford bank, alarmed at news that a creditor, Ward Larabee, was dead and exposed as a criminal. With Huachuco gone and many mouths to feed, Judy refused to leave her father as long as she could be of help. All day Sunday and most of Monday she and her guest, Altagracia, cooked for and waited on hungry men.

★ ★ ★

Twenty-four miles to the west, in Tucson, forty bars and cantinas hummed with talk about the siege of the Circle C. There were fantastic exaggerations. Some said that the Earps and Doc Holliday had taken part in it. Some even said that in addition to the Benson payroll loot, most of the money robbed from a pack train of peaceful Mexican traders, at Fronteras across the border, had also been dug up at Larabee's Cienega Creek cache. In the *Barrio Libre* many a wine glass was raised to celebrate the wiping out of the *sin verguenzas*. No more would the shameless ones prey upon their kindred coming up from Sonora.

Sunday went by and Monday. Monday night the town had never been noisier. All the usual night sounds filled the air. Dogs barked, horses whinnied, mules brayed. Windmills kept up their wheezy creakings while Mexican swains serenaded their *lindas*. Saloons and gaming rooms and beer gardens were loud with talk, sometimes with quarrelsome bursts followed by gunfire. Trains pounded by on the Southern Pacific and freight wagons churned dust on the *camino real.*

One of the milder sounds which came just after midnight was made by trotting horses and the wheels of a buckboard. Two saddle horses tied to the endgate, one of them a white-stockinged roan, came trotting along behind. The buckboard rolled into town from the east with Lynn O'Hara driving. The girl on the front seat with him had red hair and was wide awake. The one on the back seat with Roger Niles had dark hair and was soundly asleep with her head on Roger's shoulder. It had been a long tiring ride from the Circle C.

'I can hardly believe,' Judy said as they turned into the south end of Convent Street, 'that it was only four weeks ago tonight.'

'What happened four weeks ago tonight?' Lynn asked absently.

'It was then that Gracie looked out her window at Calabasas.'

'Let's forget Calabasas and think of Miss Silva. We're busting all her rules wide open.'

'But it wasn't our fault,' Judy protested, 'that the horse cast a shoe.' One of the buckboard team had lost a shoe on the way in and they'd had to hunt up a blacksmith at Papago station. Re-shoeing the hoof had delayed them three hours. Otherwise they would have arrived in town by nine o'clock.

'Since we're this late,' Lynn concluded philosophically, 'it won't hurt to be a few minutes later.' As he pulled the team to a slow walk he took the reins in one hand and slipped his free arm around Judy. 'Did I tell you the deal I cooked up with Mr. Hudson of the bank this morning?'

'Part of it,' Judy said. 'Tell it again.'

'Seems they've got a mortgage on the L Bar, every hoof horn and acre. So they're taking over. Mr. Hudson hired me for the next three months to run the place, finish the roundup and sell off enough beef to pay the due interest. At the end of three months if I like the layout they offer to deed it to me for the face of Larabee's note.'

'And what did you say?'

'I said I'd ask the girl I want to marry if she'd like to live there. Would you, Judy?'

She looked over her shoulder at the back seat. Gracie was still asleep. 'Hadn't we better wake her up?'

'Don't change the subject. Would you, Judy?'

May I have three weeks to think about it?'

Why three weeks?'

'Because in three weeks Dad'll be taking me home for another week end. You'll be stopping by, perhaps?'

'Why not?' Lynn agreed. 'I'll be your nearest neighbor by then.' Judy had settled back snugly against his arm and he was content.

He drove on down Convent Street, stopping in front of a select school for young ladies. A rank smell of hollyhocks came from beyond a picket fence. The school was dark. All of its inmates, pupils and teachers, had retired hours ago.

Lynn stood on the carriage block and handed Judy out of the rig. By now

Roger Niles had wakened Altagracia and they too got out on the walk. Lynn took Judy's satchel and Roger took Gracie's.

They passed through a picket gate and moved apprehensively up a brick path toward the school door. 'Here's where we catch it!' Roger said, foreseeing a stern Miss Silva.

At this hour the door was sure to be locked. Lynn rattled the knocker and there was a long wait. He had to rattle it again before he heard someone coming down the stairs.

The door opened and Miss Silva, in dressing gown and slippers, stood there with a candle in her hand,

'We're sorry to be so late,' Judy said.

There was no explosion. Every rule of this strictest of private schools had been shattered. Yet Miss Silva stood there with her candle and looked at them not only with forgiveness but with a hint of pride on her face. She'd read the news accounts of the Circle C's siege.

'Thank you, gentlemen.' One by one she took the satchels and set them inside the door.

Lynn touched the tip of Judy's fingers. 'Goodnight, Judy.'

Roger touched the tip of Altagracia's. 'Goodnight, Gracie.'

As the girls passed into the hallway Miss Silva raised her candle a little higher.

'Goodnight, gentlemen.' Her tone was kindly but final. The night was dark and heavy with the scent of hollyhocks as they went back to the rig and got in. Lynn took the reins but he let the team rest there a minute longer. Down on the Church Plaza a bell sounded a half hour past midnight. 'Did she say yes?' Roger asked slyly.

'She didn't say no.' Lynn's answer was under his breath and only his own singing heart heard it. He looked at dark upper windows and saw one of them suddenly brighten as a lamp was lighted inside. His whole life had brightened like that, these last few hours.

'It's Gracie's window,' Roger whispered. 'The one she spotted Larabee from.'

Lynn barely heard him. 'Sweet dreams, Judy.' He tipped his hat to the lamp glow, then shook the reins and drove on.

# HOUSTON'S STORY

## Abe Dancer

George Houston's line of work carries with it infamy and danger, and it's not long before his peaceable ride through Utah is cut dramatically short. After a bank robbery and the killing of one of its leading businessmen, the town of Bullhead is angry and wound up. But Agnes Jarrow believes it's not the work of the young hothead who breaks free from the town jail — so Houston sets off on a perilous search for Billy Carrick.

# THE WELDING QUIRT

## Max Brand

A young boy invades a camp of slumbering outlaws, and manages to create so much havoc that he routs all but one of them . . . Sleeper and his chestnut stallion Careless are rescued from a flash flood by a man named Bones. When Bones is captured by a sheriff's posse for killing two claim-jumpers, it's time for Sleeper to return the favor . . . Driven from his hometown, Snoozer Mell chooses the life of a gambler. But he has to return — and his past will pursue him . . .

# RED RIVER STAGE

## Fred Grove

Emily Bragg, captive of the Comanches, has been with them for years. When a new prisoner is brought to the camp, she befriends and protects her. But when a Comanchero promises to ransom both women, Emily is not sure she wants to leave ... When the Penateka Comanches discover the creatures ridden by the invading Spaniards, they wonder if they too could mount them ... And a fugitive on a stage bound for Indian territory finds out that his fellow passenger is a U.S. marshal ...

# VULTURE WINGS

## Dirk Hawkman

Infamous low-lives, the Strong brothers will do anything for a quick buck — but this is going to be no ordinary kidnap. They are paid to abduct two young men, and don't ask too many questions when their paymaster gives them some unusual instructions. Then, as the boys' father races to rescue his sons, he realises that their snatching is linked to dark secrets from his old life as a bounty hunter.